Michael Moorcock is astonishing. His enormous output includes around fifty novels, innumerable short stories and a rock album. Born in London in 1939, he became editor of *Tarzan Adventures* at sixteen, moving on later to edit the *Sexton Blake Library*. He has earned his living as a writer/editor ever since, and is without doubt one of Britain's most popular and most prolific authors. He has been compared with Tennyson, Tolkien, Raymond Chandler, Wyndham Lewis, Ronald Firbank, Mervyn Peake, Edgar Allan Poe, Colin Wilson, Anatole France, William Burroughs, Edgar Rice Burroughs, Charles Dickens, James Joyce, Vladimir Nabokov, Jorge Luis Borges, Joyce Cary, Ray Bradbury, H. G. Wells, George Bernard Shaw and Hieronymus Bosch, among others.

'No one at the moment in England is doing more to break down the artificial divisions that have grown up in novel writing – realism, surrealism, science fiction, historical fiction, social satire, the poetic novel – than Michael Moorcock'
Angus Wilson

'He is an ingenious and energetic experimenter, restlessly original, brimming over with clever ideas'
Robert Nye, *The Guardian*

By the same author

MICHAEL MOORCOCK

The Black Corridor

GRANADA

London Toronto Sydney New York

Published by Granada Publishing Limited in 1969
Reprinted 1970, 1973, 1975, 1980, 1982

ISBN 0 583 11640 X

Copyright © Michael Moorcock 1969

Granada Publishing Limited
Frogmore, St Albans, Herts AL2 2NF
and
36 Golden Square, London W1R 4AH
866 United Nations Plaza, New York, NY 10017, USA
117 York Street, Sydney, NSW 2000, Australia
100 Skyway Avenue, Rexdale, Ontario, M9W 3A6, Canada
61 Beach Road, Auckland, New Zealand

Printed and bound in Great Britain by
Cox & Wyman Ltd, Reading
Set in Monotype Times

Granada ®
Granada Publishing ®

Dedication:

For Hilary—
who did more than help

CHAPTER ONE

Space is neutral.

Space is infinite.
It is dark.

It is cold.

*

Stars occupy minute areas of space. They are clustered a few billion here.   A few billion there.   As if seeking consolation in numbers.

Space does not care.

*

Space does not threaten.
                    Space does not comfort.
    It does not sleep; it does not wake; it does not dream; it does not hope; it does not fear; it does not love; it does not hate; it does not encourage any of these qualities.
    Space cannot be measured. It cannot be angered. It cannot be placated. It cannot be summed up.
    Space is there.

*

Space is not large and it is not small. It does not live and it does not die. It does not offer truth and neither does it lie.
    Space is a remorseless, senseless, impersonal fact.
    Space is the absence of time and of matter.

*

Through this silence moves a tiny pellet of metal. It moves so slowly as to seem not to move at all. It is a lonely little object. In its own terms it is a long way from its planet of origin.
    In the solid blackness it gives off faint light. In that great life-denying void it contains life.
    A few wisps of gas hang on it; a certain amount of its own waste matter surrounds it: cans and packages and bits of paper, globules of fluid, things rejected by its system as beyond reconstitution. They cling to its sides for want of anything better to cling to.
    And inside the spacecraft is Ryan.

Ryan is dressed neatly in regulation coveralls which are light grey in colour and tend to match the vast expanse of controls, predominantly grey and green, which surround him. Ryan himself is pale and his hair is mainly grey. He might have been designed to tone in with the ship.

Ryan is a tall man with heavy grey-black eyebrows that meet near the bridge of his nose. He has grey eyes and full, firm lips that are at the moment pressed tightly together. He seems physically very fit. Ryan knows that he has to keep himself in shape.

*

Ryan paces the spaceship. He paces down the central passageway to the main control cabin and there he checks the coordinates, the consumption indicators, the regeneration indicators and he checks all his figures, at length, with those of the ship's computer.

He is quietly satisfied.

Everything is perfectly in order; exactly as it should be.

Ryan goes to the desk near the ship's big central screen. Although activated, the screen shows no picture. It casts a greenish light on to the desk. Ryan sits down and reaches out towards the small console on the desk. He depresses a stud and, speaking in a clear, level voice, he makes his standard log entry:

'Day number one thousand, four hundred and sixty three. Spaceship *Hope Dempsey* en route for Munich 15040. Speed holds steady at point nine of *c*. All systems functioning according to original expectations. No other variations. We are all comfortable.

'Signing off.

'Ryan, Acting Commander.'

The entry will be filed in the ship's records and will also be automatically broadcast back to Earth.

Now Ryan slides open a drawer and takes from it a large red book. It is his personal log-book. He unclips a stylus from a pocket in his coveralls, scratches his head and writes, slowly and carefully. He puts down the date: December 24th, A.D. 2005. He takes another stylus from his pocket and underlines this date in red. He looks up at the blank screen and seems to make a decision.

He writes:

The silence of these infinite spaces frightens me.

He underlines the phrase in red

He writes:

I am lonely. I am controlling a desperate longing. Yet I know that it is not my function to feel lonely. I almost wish for an emergency so that I could wake at least one of them up.

8

Mr Ryan pulls himself together. He takes a deep breath and be gins a more formal entry, the third of his eight-hourly reports.

When he has finished, he gets up, puts the red log-book away, replaces his stylii neatly in his pocket, goes over to the main console and makes a few fine adjustments to the instruments.

He leaves the main control cabin, enters a short companion way, opens a door.

He is in his living quarters. It is a small compartment and very tidy. On one wall is a console with a screen that shows him the interior of the main control cabin. Set in the opposite wall is a double bunk.

He undresses, disposes of his coveralls, lies down and takes a sedative. He sleeps. His breathing is heavy and regular at first.

*

He goes into the ballroom. It is dusk. There are long windows looking out on to a darkening lawn. The floor gleams; the lights overhead are dim.

On the ballroom floor formally dressed couples slowly rotate in perfect time to the music. The music is low and rather sombre. All the couples wear round, very black spectacles. Their faces are pale, their features almost invisible in the dim light. The round black glasses give them a masklike appearance.

Around the floor other couples are sitting out. They stare forward through their dark glasses. As the couples move the music becomes quieter and quieter, slower and slower, and now the couples revolve more slowly too.

The music fades.

Now a low psalmlike moaning begins. It is in the room but it does not come from the dancers.

The mood in the room changes.

At last the dancers stand perfectly still, listening to the song. The seated men and women stand up. The chanting grows louder. The people in the room become angry. They are angry with a particular individual. Above the chanting, louder and faster, comes the beating of a rapid drum.

The dancers are angry, angry, angry . . .

Ryan awakes and remembers the past.

CHAPTER TWO

Ryan and Mrs Ryan shyly entered their new apartment and laid down the large nearly brand-new suitcase. It came to rest on the floor of the lobby. They released the handle. The suitcase rocked and then was still.

Ryan's attention left the case and focused on the shining tub in which grew a diminutive orange tree.

'Mother's kept it well watered,' murmured Mrs Ryan.

'Yes,' said Ryan.

'She's very good about things like that.'

'Yes.'

Awkwardly Ryan took her in his arms. Mrs Ryan embraced him. There was a certain reserve in her movements as if she were frightened of him or of the consequences her action might provoke.

A feeling of tenderness overwhelmed Ryan. He smiled down at her upturned face, reached out his hand to stroke her jawline. She smiled uncertainly.

'Well,' he said. 'Let's inspect the family mansion.'

Hand in hand they wandered through the apartment, over the pale gold carpets, past the simulated oak furniture of the living-room to stare out through the long window at the apartment blocks opposite.

'Not too close,' said Ryan with satisfaction. 'Wouldn't it be terrible to live like the Benedicts — so near the next block that you can see right into their rooms. And they can see right into yours.'

'Awful,' agreed Mrs Ryan. 'No privacy. No privacy at all.'

They wandered past the wall-to-wall television into the kitchen. They opened cupboards and surveyed the contents. They pressed buttons to slide out the washing machine and the refrigerator. They turned on the infragrill, played with the telephone, touched the walls. They went into the two empty bedrooms, looking out of the windows, turning on the lights, their feet noisy on the tiles of the floors.

Last of all they went into the main bedroom, where the coloured lights of the walls shifted idly in the bright sunshine from the windows. They opened the wardrobes in which their clothes had been neatly laid out.

Mrs Ryan patted her hair in front of the huge convex mirror opposite the bed. Shyly they stood, looking out of the window.

Ryan pressed the button on the sill and the blinds slid down.

'Aren't the walls beautiful.' Mrs Ryan turned to look at the multicoloured lights playing over the flat surfaces.

'Not as beautiful as you.'

She looked round at him. 'Oh, you . . .'

Ryan reached out and touched her shoulder, touched her left breast, touched her waist.

Mrs Ryan glanced at the windows as if to reassure herself that the blinds were drawn and no one could see in.

'Oh, I'm so happy,' she whispered.

'So am I.' Ryan moved closer, drew her to him, holding her buttocks cupped in his heavy hands. He kissed her lightly on the nose, then strongly on the mouth. His hand left her buttock and moved down her thigh, pushing up the skirt, feeling her flesh.

A flush came to Mrs Ryan's face as he eased her towards the new bed. She opened her lips and stroked the back of his neck. She sighed.

His thumb traced the line of her pelvis. She trembled and moved against him.

Then the Chinese jazz record started in the next apartment. The Ryans froze. Mrs Ryan was bent backwards with Mr Ryan's face buried in her neck. The clangour of the record, every note and every phrase, was as audible as if the music poured from their own glowing walls.

They broke apart. Mrs Ryan straightened her skirt.

'Damn them!' Mr Ryan raised his fists impotently. 'Good God! Don't tell me that's the kind of neighbours we've got.'

'Hadn't you better . . . ?'

'What?'

'Couldn't you . . . ?' She was confused.

'You mean . . . ?'

'. . . go and speak to them?'

'Well, I . . .' He frowned. 'Maybe this time I'll just hammer on the wall.'

Slowly he took off his shoe. 'I'll show them.' He went to the wall and banged on it vigorously, stood back, shoe in hand, and waited.

The music stopped.

He grinned. 'That did it.'

Mrs Ryan took a deep breath and said, 'I'd better unpack.'

'I'll help you,' said Ryan.

He left the bedroom and approached the suitcase. He took the handle in both hands and staggered back to where she was waiting.

Together they unpacked the residue of their honeymoon — the suntan lotions, the damp bathing suits, the tissue-wrapped gifts for

11

their parents. They talked and they laughed as they took things out of the case and put them away, but secretly they were sad as article after article came out. All the souvenirs of that sunny three weeks on an island where no one else lived, where there was freedom from observation, the noise and demands of other people.

The case was empty.

Mrs Ryan reached into the waterproof pouch at the back and produced the tapes they had had processed when they reached the mainland heliport. He fetched the player from the dressing table and they went into the living-room to play the tapes on the television.

In silence they looked at the pictures, drinking in the landscapes they showed. There were the mountains, there the great blue expanse of the sea, there the heaths.

There were almost no shots of Mr or Mrs Ryan. There were only the views of the silent crags, the sea and the moors of the island where they had been so happy.

A bird cried.

Somewhat shakily the picture swept upwards towards the cloud-slashed sky. A kittyhawk dived into the distance. There was the sound of the breakers in the background.

Suddenly the picture cut out.

Mrs Ryan looked at Mr Ryan with tears in her eyes.

'We must go back there soon,' she said.

'Very soon,' he smiled.

And the Chinese jazz, as loud as ever, shrieked through the room.

The Ryans sat rigidly in front of the television screen.

Ryan clenched his teeth. 'Jesus God, I'll . . .' he stood up . . . 'I'll kill the bastards!' He gestured irresolutely. 'There are laws. I'll call the police.'

Mrs Ryan held his hand. 'There's no need to speak to them, darling. Just put a note through their door. Warn them. They must have heard of the Noise Prevention Act. You could write to the caretaker as well.'

Ryan rubbed his lips once.

'Tell them they could be heavily fined,' said his wife. 'If they're reasonable, they'll . . .'

'All right.' Ryan pursed his lips. 'This time that's what I'll do. Next time — and I mean it — I'll knock on the door and confront them.'

He went into the living room to write the notes. Mrs Ryan made tea.

The Chinese jazz went on and on. Ryan wrote the notes with short, jerky movements of his pen.

. . . and I warn you that if this noise continues I will be forced to contact the police and inform them of your conduct. I have also told the caretaker of my intention. At very least you will be evicted — but you must also be aware of the heavy penalties you could receive under Section VII of the Noise Prevention Act of 1978.

He read back over the letter. It was a bit pompous. He hesitated. Perhaps if he . . . ? No. It would do. He finished the letters, put them into envelopes and sealed them as Mrs Ryan directed the tea trolley into the living-room. 'That will do, thank you,' she told it.

Suddenly the music stopped in mid-bar. Ryan looked at his wife and laughed. 'Maybe that's the answer? Maybe it's robots making that row?'

Mrs Ryan smiled. She picked up the tea-pot.

'Look, I'll do that,' said Ryan, 'if you'll just put these into the internal mail slot outside the front door.'

'All right.' Mrs Ryan replaced the pot. 'But what shall I do if I meet them?' She nodded towards the neighbouring flat.

'Ignore them completely, of course. They surely won't try to involve you in conversation. You might as well ignore anybody else you meet outside. If we start making contact with all the people in this block we'll never have any bloody privacy.'

'That's what Mother said,' said Mrs Ryan.

'Right.'

She took the two letters and went out of the living room and into the lobby. Ryan heard the front door click open.

He straightened his head as he heard another voice. It was a woman's voice, high-pitched and cheerful. He heard Mrs Ryan mumble something, heard her footsteps as she entered hastily and shut the front door firmly.

'What on earth was that?' he asked as she returned to the living room. 'It's like living in a zoo. Maybe it was a mistake . . .'

'It was the woman who lives on the other side of us. She was coming back with her shopping. She welcomed me to the block. I said thank you very much and slid back in here.'

'Oh, Christ, I hope they're not going to pester us,' said Ryan.

'I don't think so. She seemed quite embarrassed to be chatting with a stranger.'

In cosy, uninterrupted silence the Ryans drank their tea and ate their sandwiches and cake.

When they had finished Mrs Ryan ordered the trolley back to the kitchen and she and Ryan sat together on the couch watching the tapes on the television. They were beginning to feel at ease in their little home.

Mrs Ryan smiled at the screen and pointed. There was a scene of cliffs, a cave. 'Remember that old fisherman we found in there that day? I was never so startled in my life. You said ——'

A steady knocking began.

Ryan swung round, seeking the source of the noise.

'Over here,' said a voice.

Ryan got up. Outside the window was the head and torso of a man in overalls. His grinning red face was capped by a mop of clashing ginger hair. His teeth were ragged and yellow.

Mrs Ryan put her hand to her mouth as Ryan dashed to the window.

'What the bloody hell do you think you're doing, pushing your fucking face in our window without warning?' Ryan trembled with rage. 'What's the matter with you? Haven't you ever heard of privacy? Can't we get a moment's peace and quiet? It's a bloody conspiracy!'

The man's grin faded as Ryan ranted on. His muffled voice came through the pane. 'Look here,' he said. 'There's no need to be like that. I never knew you was back, did I? I was asked by the old lady to keep the windows clean while you was away. Which I have done without, if I may say so, any payment whatsoever. So before you complain about my bloody habits, I suggest you settle up . . .'

'How much?' Ryan put his hand in his pocket. 'Come on — how much?'

'Three pounds seven.'

Ryan opened the window and put four pound notes on the outside sill. 'There you are. Keep the change. And while you're at it don't bother to come back. We don't need you. I'm going to clean the windows myself.'

The man grinned cynically. 'Oh, yeah?' He tucked the money into his overall pocket. 'I hope you've got a head for heights, then. They're all telling me they're going to clean their own windows from now on. Have you seen them? Half of them don't do the outsides. They can't stand the height, see? You should see 'em. Filthy. You can hardly see out for the dirt. It must be like the black hole of Calcutta in most of them flats. Still, it's none of my business, I'm sure. If people want to live in the dark that's their affair, not mine.'

'Too right,' said Ryan. 'You nosy bloody . . .'

The window-cleaner's eyes hardened. 'Look, mate . . .'

'Clear off,' said Ryan fiercely. 'Go on!'

The man shrugged, gave his yellow grin again and touched his

14

carroty hair sardonically in a salute. 'Cheerio, then, smiler.' He began to lower himself down the wall towards the distant ground.

Ryan turned to look at his wife. Mrs Ryan was not on the couch any more. He heard sobs and followed the sound.

Mrs Ryan was stretched across the bed, face down, weeping hysterically.

He touched her shoulder. 'Cheer up, love. He's gone now.'

She shrugged off his hand.

'Cheer up. I'll . . .'

'I've always been a *private* person,' she cried. 'It's all right for you — you weren't brought up like me. People in our neighbourhood never intruded. They didn't come poking their faces through windows. Why did you bring me here? *Why?*'

'Darling, I find it all just as distasteful as you do,' Ryan told her. 'Honestly. We'll just have to sort it out step by step. Show people that we like to keep ourselves to ourselves. Be calm.'

Mrs Ryan continued to cry.

'Please don't cry, darling.' Mr Ryan ran his hands through his hair. 'I'll straighten things out. You won't see anyone you don't know.'

She turned on the bed. 'I'm sorry . . . One thing after another. My nerves . . .'

'I know.'

He sat down on the edge of the bed and began to stroke her hair. 'Come on. We'll watch a musical on the TV. Then we'll . . .'

And as Mrs Ryan's sobs abated there came the familiar sound of the Chinese jazz. It was muted now, but it was still loud enough to lacerate the Ryans' sensitive ears.

Mrs Ryan moaned and covered her head as the tinkling, the jangling, the thudding of the music beat against her.

Ryan, helpless, stood and stared down at his weeping wife.

Then he turned and began to bang and bang and bang and bang on the wall until all the colours disappeared.

But the music kept on playing.

CHAPTER THREE

Mr Ryan has done his exercises, bathed, dressed and breakfasted.

He has left his cabin and has paced down the main passageway to the central control cabin. He has checked the coordinates, the consumption indicators, the regeneration indicators and run computations through the machine.

He seats himself at the tidy steel desk below the big screen that has no picture. Around him the dials and the indicators move unobtrusively.

Mr Ryan takes out the heavy red-covered log-book from its steel drawer. He unclips his pen.

Using the old-fashioned log appeals to his imagination, his sense of pioneerdom. It is the one touch of the historic, the link with the great captains and explorers of the past. The log-book is Ryan's poem.

He enters the date: December 25th, A.D. 2005. He underlines it. He begins to write the first of his eight-hourly reports:

Day number one thousand, four hundred and sixty four. Spaceship Hope Dempsey en route for Munich 15040. Speed steady at point nine of c. All systems functioning according to original expectations. No other variations. All occupants are comfortable and in good health.

Under this statement Ryan signs his name and rules a neat line. He then stands up and reads the entry into the machine.

Ryan's report is on its way to Earth.

He likes to vary this routine. Therefore when he makes his next report he will do it orally first and write it second.

Ryan stands up, checks the controls, glances around and is satisfied that all is in order. Since embarkation on the *Hope Dempsey* three years ago he has lost weight and, in spite of his treatments under the lamps, colour. Ryan exercises and eats well and relatively speaking he is in the best possible condition for a man living at two-thirds Earth gravity. On Earth it would be doubtful if he could run a hundred yards, walk along the corridor of a train, move a table from one side of a room to another. His muscles are maintained, but they have forgotten much. And Ryan's mind, basically still the same, has also forgotten much in the narrow confines of the perfectly running ship.

But Ryan has his will. His will makes him keep to the perfect routine which will take the ship and its occupants to the star. That will which has held Ryan, the ship and its instruments and passengers together for three years, and will hold them together, functioning correctly, for the next three.

Ryan trusts his will.

Thus, in the private and unofficial section of the red log-book, the section which is never read over to Earth, Ryan writes:

Today is Alex's tenth birthday — another birthday he will miss. This is very saddening. However it is the kind of sacrifice we must make for ourselves and for others in our attempt to make a better life. I find myself increasingly lonely for the company of my dear wife and children and my other old friends and good companions. Broadcasts from Earth no longer reach us and soon I shall be reduced, for stimulation, to those old shipmates of mine, my videotapes, my audio-tapes and my books. But all this must be if we are to achieve our end — to gain anything worthwhile demands endurance and discipline. In three minutes it will be time to perform the duty I find most painful emotionally — and yet most essential. Every day I am seized by the same mixture of reluctance, because I know the distress it will cause me. And yet there is an eagerness to fulfill my task. I shall go now and do what I have to.

Ryan closes the red log-book and places it back in the steel drawer so that the near edges of the book rest evenly against the bottom of the drawer. He replaces his pen in his pocket and stands up. He glances once more at the controls and with a firm step leaves the room.

He walks up the metallic central corridor of the ship. At the end there is a door. The door is secured by heavy spin screws. Ryan presses a button at the side of the door and the screws automatically retract. The door swings open and Ryan stands for a moment on the threshold.

The room is a small one, instantly bright as the heavy door opens. There are no screens to act as portholes and the walls gleam with a platinum sheen.

The room is empty except for the thirteen long containers.

One of the containers is empty. Plastic sheets are drawn two-thirds of the way up over the twelve full containers. Through the semi-transparent material covering the remainder of the tops can be seen a thick, dark green fluid. Through the fluid can be seen the faces and shoulders of the passengers.

The passengers are in hibernation and will remain so until the ship lands (unless an emergency arises which will be important enough for Ryan to awaken them). In their gallons of green fluid they sleep.

At their heads is a panel revealing the active working of their bodies. On the plastic cover is a small identification panel, giving their names, their dates of birth and the date of their engulfment into suspended animation. On the indicator panel is a line marked

DREAMS. On each panel the line is steady.

Ryan looks tenderly down into the faces of his family and friends.

JOSEPHINE RYAN. 9.9.1960. 7.3.2004. His wife. Blonde and plump-faced, her naked shoulders still pink and smooth.

*

RUPERT RYAN. 13.7.1990. 6.3.2004. The dark face of his son, so like his, the bony shoulders just beginning to broaden into manhood.

*

ALEXANDER RYAN. 25.12.1996. 6.3.2004. The fairer face of his younger son. Eyes, amazingly, still open. So blue. Thin shoulders of an active small boy.

*

Ryan, looking on the faces of his closest relatives, feels close to tears at their loss. But he controls himself and paces past the other containers.

*

SYDNEY RYAN. 2.2.1937. 25.12.2003. His uncle. An old man. False teeth, very white, revealed through open mouth. Eyes closed. Thin, wrinkled shoulders.

*

JOHN RYAN. 15.8.1963. 26.12.2003. Ryan's brother. Ryan thinks that now he is thinner, less muscular, he must look more like John than he has ever done, even when they were children. John has the same short face, thick brows. His exposed shoulders are narrow, knotted.

*

ISABEL RYAN. 22.6.1962. 13.2.2004. His brother John's first wife, her crowded teeth exposed in a snarl in her narrow jaw. Pale face, pale hair, pale, thin shoulders. Ryan feels a spasm of relief that Isabel is lying in her container instead of around him, erect and needlelike, talking to him in her high voice. Ryan does not notice the passing thought, does not need to correct himself.

*

JANET RYAN. 10.11.1982. 7.5.2004. So lovely. His brother John's second wife. Soft cheeks, soft shoulders, long wavy black hair suspended in the green fluid, a gentle smile through pink, generous lips, as if she were dreaming pleasant dreams.

*

FRED MASTERSON. 4.5.1950. 25.12.2003. Narrow face. Thin, narrow shoulders. Furrowed brow.

*

TRACY MASTERSON. 29.10.1973. 9.10.2003. Masterson's wife. A pretty woman, looking as stupid in her container as she did out of it.

*

JAMES HENRY. 4.3.1957. 29.10.2003. Shock of red hair floating, sea-green eyes open in the green fluid. Looking like some drowned merman.

*

Ryan moves past him and stops at the eleventh container.

*

IDA HENRY. 3.3.1980. 1.2.2004. Poor girl. Matted hair, pale brown. Sunken young cheeks, drooping mouth.

*

There are two arrested lives in that container, Ryan thought. Ida, Henry's wife, and her coming child. What would be the result of that long gestation of mother and child, both in foetal fluid.

*

FELICITY HENRY. 3.3.1980. 1.2.2004. Henry's other wife and Ida's twin sister. Her hair is smoother and shinier, her cheeks less sunken than her sister's. Not pregnant.

*

Ryan reaches the last container and looks into it. The white bottom of the container shines up at him. Surrounded by his sleeping companions he has the urge to get into the container and try it out.

Suspecting his impulse, he squares his shoulders and walks firmly from the room. The door hisses shut behind him. He touches the stud that replaces the screws. He walks back down the silent corridor and re-enters the control cabin. He makes rapid notes on a small pad of paper he takes from his breast pocket. He moves to the computer and runs his calculations through.

If necessary the computer could be switched to fully automatic, but this is not considered good for the psychology of crew members.

Ryan nods with satisfaction when the replies come. He returns to the desk and puts the charts back in the drawer.

As he does this another spurt of paper comes from the computer. Ryan examines it.

It reads:

REPORT ON PERSONNEL IN CONTAINERS NOT SUPPLIED.
Ryan purses his lips and punches in the reports:

JOSEPHINE RYAN.	CONDITION STEADY
RUPERT RYAN.	CONDITION STEADY
ALEXANDER RYAN.	CONDITION STEADY
SIDNEY RYAN.	CONDITION STEADY
JOHN RYAN.	CONDITION STEADY
ISABEL RYAN.	CONDITION STEADY
JANET RYAN.	CONDITION STEADY
FRED MASTERSON.	CONDITION STEADY
TRACY MASTERSON.	CONDITION STEADY
JAMES HENRY.	CONDITION STEADY
IDA HENRY.	CONDITION STEADY
FELICITY HENRY.	CONDITION STEADY *******

****
*******YOUR OWN CONDITION
suggests the computer.
Ryan pauses and then reports:
I AM LONELY
The computer tells him instantly:
*******FILL YOUR TIME ACCORDING TO THE SUGGESTED PROGRAMME. IF THE CONDITION CONTINUES INJECT ICC PRODITOL PER DIEM * DO NOT TAKE MORE * DISCONTINUE THE DOSAGE AS SOON AS POSSIBLE AND AT ALL COSTS AFTER 14 DAYS****

Ryan straightens his shoulders, signs off and walks away from the computer.

He walks down the corridor to his own accommodation. He

inflates a red easy chair, sits down and presses a stud on the wall. The TV screen in front of him begins to roll off a list of its offerings. Films, plays, music, dancing and discussion and educational programmes. In his weakness Ryan does not choose the agricultural information he is committed to studying. He selects an old Polish film.

Soon the screen is full of people walking, talking, eating, getting on streetcars, watching scenery, kissing and arguing.

Ryan feels tears on his cheeks but he has an hour of relaxation due to him and he will take it, in whatever form it comes.

As Ryan watches, bearing his expected melancholy with stoicism, his mind wanders. He hears, echoing in his head, the report on his undead companions in their cavernous containers: JOSEPHINE RYAN. CONDITION STEADY. RUPERT RYAN. CONDITION STEADY. ALEXANDER RYAN . . . SIDNEY RYAN . . . JOHN RYAN . . . ISABEL RYAN . . . JANET RYAN . . . FRED MASTERSON . . . JAMES HENRY . . . IDA HENRY . . . FELICITY HENRY . . .

The parade of the faces he once knew passes in front of him. He imagines them as they were, before they were immersed in their half-life in the sea-green fluid.

CHAPTER FOUR

James Henry's pale hands, stubby and freckled, shook as he bent forward in his chair and stared into Fred Masterson's face.

'*Do* something, Fred, *do* something — that's what I'm saying.'

Masterson gazed back, thin eyebrows raised cynically, long forehead creased by parallels of wrinkles. 'Such as?' he asked after a pause.

Henry's hands clenched as he said: 'Society is polluted physically and morally. Polluted by radioactivity we're continually told is within an acceptable level — though we see signs every day that this just isn't so. I cannot allow Ida or Felicity to bear children with the world as it is today. And worse, in a way, than the actual environment is the infinite corruption of man himself. Each day we grow more rotten, like sacks of pus, until the few of us who try to cling to the old standards, try to stay decent, are more and more threatened by the others. Threatened by their corruption, threatened by their violence. We're living in a mad world, Masterson, and you're advising patience . . .'

Beside him on the Ryans' couch were his two wives, tired, identically pale, identically thin, as if the split cell which produced them had only contained the materials for one healthy woman and had been forced to make two. As Henry spoke they both gazed at him from their pale blue eyes and followed every word as if he were speaking their thoughts.

Masterson did not reply to James Henry's tirade. He merely stared about him as if he were thoroughly tired of the discussion.

The furniture of the Ryans' living room had been pushed back against the walls to seat the group which met there every week.

The blinds were drawn and the lights were on.

Seated on his own with his back to the window was Ryan's Uncle Sidney, a thin, obstinate old man with a tonsure of brown hair round his bald head. The rest of the group was seated around the other walls. The seat in front of the window, like the front row at public meetings, was always the last to be filled.

Fred Masterson and his wife Tracy, who wore a well-cut black floor-length dress, the conservative fashion of the moment, and fully made up black lips, sat opposite the Henry family on their sofa.

Next to Masterson sat John Ryan's first wife, Isabel. She was a dowdy, pinch-faced woman. On John's left sat his other wife, the beautiful Janet. Against the fourth wall were Ryan and his wife Josephine.

The women wore blacks and browns, the men were quietly dressed in dark-coloured tunics and trousers. The room, bare in the centre, entirely without ornament, had a dull look.

Ryan sat and in his head worked out some estimates for a new line of product in his head. As a silence fell between James Henry and Fred Masterson, he turned his mind away from his business problems and said:

'This is, after all, only a discussion group. We haven't the power or the means to alter things.'

Henry opened his green eyes wider and said urgently:

'Can't you see, Ryan, that the days of discussion are practically over. We're living in chaos and all we're doing is talking about it. At the meeting next month —— '

'We haven't agreed to a meeting next month yet,' said Masterson.

'Well, if we don't we'll be fools.' Henry crossed his legs in an agitated manner. 'At the meeting next month we must urge that pressure . . .'

Tracy Masterson's face was taut with stress. 'I've got to go home now, Fred.

Masterson looked at her helplessly. 'Try to hang on . . .'

'No . . .' Tracy hunched her shoulders. 'No. It's people all around me. I know they're all friends . . . I know they don't mean to . . .'

'A couple more minutes.'

'No. It's like being shut up in a box.'

She folded her hands in her lap and sat with her eyes downcast. She could say no more.

Josephine Ryan rose and took her by the arm. 'I'll give you some pills and you can sleep in our bed. Come on, dear . .' She drew the younger woman up by the arm and led her into the kitchen.

Henry looked at Masterson. 'Well? You know why your wife is like this. It all dates from the time when she was caught up in that UFO Demonstration in Powell Square. And that's an experience any one of us could have at any time — as things are now.'

As he spoke there came the sound of chanting from nearby streets. A window broke in the distance and there were shouts. A noisy song began.

From the bedroom Tracy Masterson started to scream.

Fred Masterson got up, paused for a moment and then ran towards the sound.

The rest of the group sat frozen, listening as the hubbub came closer. In the bedroom Tracy Masterson screamed and shouted: 'NO. NO. NO. NO. NO. NO. NO. NO.'

Josephine Ryan came back, leaning against the doorway. 'The pills will take effect soon. Don't worry about her. Who are the people in the street?'

No one replied.

Tracy screamed again.

'Who are the people in the street?' Josephine moved further into the room. 'Who?'

The noisy voices subsided, giving way to the same low chanting, in a minor key, which had begun the procession.

Now Ryan and his friends could hear some of the words.

'Shut up the land.

'Shut up the sky.

'We must be alone.

'Strangers, strangers all must die.

'We must be alone.

'Alone, alone, alone.

'Shut out the fearful, darkening skies.

23

'Let us be alone.

'No strangers coming through the skies.

'We must be alone.

'No threats, no fears.

'No strangers here.

'No thieves who come by night.

'Alone, alone, alone.'

'It's them, then. The Patriots.' Mrs Ryan looked at the others. Again no one replied.

The chanting was close under the windows now.

The lights went out. The room was left in complete darkness.

Tracy Masterson's screams had diminished to a whimper as the drug took hold.

'Bloody awful verses, whatever else . . .' Uncle Sidney cleared his throat.

The group sat surrounded by a chanting which seemed, in the utter darkness, to be coming from all over the room.

Suddenly it stopped.

There was the sound of running and sharp cries. Then a pitiful high screaming like the sound of an animal being killed.

Uncle Sidney stirred in his chair by the window and stood up. 'Let's have a look out, then,' he said calmly. His finger went to the button on the window sill.

As James Henry shouted *No!* Ryan was halfway across the room, arms stretched toward his uncle.

It was too late.

The blind shot up.

The window covering the whole of one wall was open to the night.

Ryan stood petrified in the middle of the floor as the flickering light cast by a thousand torches in the street played over him. Henry half out of his seat, stood up and was completely still.

Josephine Ryan stood in the middle of the floor with the bottle of pills in her hand.

The dark-clad women sat in their seats without moving.

The cries and the terrible high scream went on.

Uncle Sidney looked down into the street. On the other side, in the high block opposite, all the windows were blinded.

"Oh, my God,' said Uncle Sidney. 'Oh, my God.'

There was silence until Josephine Ryan said:

'What is it?'

Uncle Sidney said nothing. He looked downwards.

24

Mrs Ryan took a deep breath. She walked firmly over to the window. Ryan watched her.

She steeled herself, looked swiftly down into the street, stepped back. 'It's too horrible. That really is too horrible.'

Uncle Sidney's face was hard. He continued to watch.

The crowd had caught a young man of twenty, one of the people who lived in the block opposite. They had tied him to an old wooden door, propped the door against a steel power supply post, drenched the door and the young man with petrol and set light to him.

The young man lay at an angle on the blazing door. He writhed and he screamed as the flames consumed him. The crowd pressed closely round, those in front being perpetually pushed too close to the flames by the people at the back who wanted to see. Their torches and the light cast over them by their human bonfire revealed chiefly men, most of them in their thirties and forties. The women among them were younger. All were dressed in dark, long clothing. In the front the people were crouched, tensely watching the young man burn.

A young woman with cropped blonde hair yelled: 'Burn, stranger, burn.' The men about her took up the cry. 'Burn, burn, burn, burn!'

The young man writhed in the flames, gave a final, frantic twist of his body and was still.

When he had stopped screaming, the crowd became quiet. Apparently they were exhausted. They sat or stood about, breathing heavily, wiping their faces and hands and mouths.

Uncle Sidney pressed the blind button in silence. The blind slid down, blotting out the torches, the fire, the silent crowd below. He sat heavily in his chair.

The crackling of the fire could be heard in the Ryan's living-room.

Mrs Ryan took her hand from her eyes, walked out to the kitchen and went to the sink. The men and women in the room heard her running water into a tumbler, heard her drink and put the tumbler into the dishwasher, heard the door of the washer close.

Uncle Sidney sat in his chair, looking at the floor.

'What did you want the blind open for?' James Henry demanded. 'Eh?'

Uncle Sidney shrugged and continued to stare at the floor.

'Eh?'

'What difference does it make?' said Uncle Sidney. 'What bloody difference . . . ?''

25

'You had no right to expose us to that — particularly the women,' said James Henry.

Uncle Sidney looked up and there were a few tears in his eyes. His voice was strained. 'It happened, didn't it?'

'What's that got to do with it? We don't want to get involved. It's not even your home. It was Josephine's window which was uncovered when — this thing — took place. She'll be the one accused!'

Uncle Sidney didn't reply. 'It happened, that's all I know. It happened — and it happened here.'

'Very horrifying to see, no doubt,' said Henry. 'But that doesn't make any difference to the fact that the Patriots have got some of the right ideas, even if they do put them into practice in a very distasteful way.' He sniffed. 'Besides — some people enjoy watching that sort of thing. Revel in it. As bad as them.'

Uncle Sidney's eyes expressed vague astonishment. 'Do what?'

'What did you want to watch it for then?'

'I didn't *want* to watch it . . .'

'So you say . . .'

Masterson appeared in the doorway and said: 'Tracy's gone to sleep at last. What's been happening? Patriots, was it?'

Ryan nodded. 'They just burnt a man. Outside. In the street.'

Masterson wrinkled his nose. 'Bloody lunatics. If they really want to get rid of them there's plenty of legal machinery to help them.'

'Quite,' said Henry. 'No need to take the law into their own hands. What bothers me is this odd anti-space notion of theirs.'

'Quite,' said Masterson. 'They've been reassured time and time again that there are no alien bodies in the skies. They've been given a dozen different kinds of proof and yet they continue to believe in an alien attack.'

'There could be some truth in it, couldn't there?' Janet said timidly. 'No smoke without fire, eh?'

The three men looked at her.

'I suppose so,' Masterson agreed. He made a dismissive gesture. 'But it's extremely unlikely.'

Mrs Ryan directed the trolley through the door. The group sat drinking coffee and eating cake.

'Drink up while it's hot.' Mrs Ryan's voice had an edge to it.

Isabel Ryan flinched and said: 'No thank you, Josephine. It doesn't agree with me.'

Josephine's mouth turned down.

'Isabel hasn't been very well,' her husband John said defensively.

Ryan tried to smooth things over. He smiled at Isabel.

'You're quite right to be careful,' he said.

The whole group knew, from Isabel's demeanour, although no one would have stated it, that Isabel was experiencing a phase where she supposed people were trying to poison her. She would eat and drink nothing she had not prepared herself.

Most of them knew what it was like. They had gone through the same thing at one time or another. It was best to ignore it.

Anyway, it wasn't unheard of for people who believed that sort of thing to be perfectly right. They all knew men and women who had imagined that they were being poisoned who later had died inexplicably.

'One of us ought to attend the next big meeting of the Patriots,' said Ryan. 'It would be interesting to know what they're up to.'

'It's dangerous.' John Ryan's face was stern.

'I'd like to know though.' Ryan shrugged. 'It's best to investigate a thing, isn't it? We ought to find out what they're really saying.'

'We'll go in a band, then,' said James Henry. 'Safety in numbers, eh?'

His wives looked at him fearfully.

'Right,' said Masterson. 'Time to tune into the report of the Nimmoite Rally at Parliament. The Government will fall tonight.'

They watched the Nimmoite Rally on the television. They watched it while more cries and shouts sounded from the street below. They watched as a group passed playing drums and pipes. They did not look round. They watched the Nimmoite Rally until the President appeared in the House of Commons and offered his resignation.

CHAPTER FIVE

That night there were riots and fires all over the city.

The Ryans and their friends watched the riots and fires, sitting behind their closed blinds, staring at the large, bright wall which was their television.

The city was being ripped and battered and bloodied.

They drank their coffee and they ate their cake and they watched the men fall under the police clubs, watched the girls and boys savaged by police dogs, heard the hooting and yelling of the looters, saw the fire service battling to control the fires.

The Ryans and their friends had seen a great many riots and fires in their lives, but never so many at a single time. They watched almost critically for a while.

But as the programmes wore on, Mrs Ryan became quieter and quieter, more mechanical in her presentation of coffee, of sugar, of things to eat.

It was when she saw her favourite department store go up in flames that she finally put her head in her arms and sobbed . . .

Mrs Ryan had been married for fourteen years.

For fourteen years she had carried the weight of her vigorous husband's moods and ambitions. She had reared children, battled with her fear of other people, of the outside, had made almost all family decisions.

She had done her best.

Now she wept.

Ryan was startled.

He went over and patted her, tried to comfort her, but she could not be stopped. She went on crying.

Ryan looked up from his wife and stared at Uncle Sidney. In front of them, unheeded, glass was smashing into the streets, crowds were running and shouting, the top of the Monument, built to commemorate the Great Fire of 1666, was crowned with flames.

'Put her to bed,' said Uncle Sidney. 'You can't do or say anything effective. It's the situation that's getting her down. Put her to bed.'

The group watched as sensible Josephine Ryan was supported out of the room by her husband. Josephine Ryan was about to be sedated and put to bed next to the unconscious Tracy Masters.

Ida and Felicity Henry, seeing their senior woman carried off, became alarmed. Ida shuddered and Felicity said: 'Where will it end?'

'You're becoming inhuman,' said Uncle Sidney. 'Switched off.'

'In the grave unless we do something fast,' James Henry said brutally. Apparently he hadn't heard Uncle Sidney.

'In the grave,' he said again. 'What are you two going to do, eh?' And he laughed nastily into the pale, identical faces of his two sapless wives.

Fred Masterson looked at Uncle Sidney and Uncle Sidney looked at Fred Masterson. They shrugged almost at the same time.

And there was Henry laughing as usual. As usual, leaning forward in his chair. As usual, springy, full of ideas, head crowned by that energetic mass of red hair which gave the impression of a man

28

getting extra fuel from somewhere.

As James Henry pushed his features aggressively towards the faces of his tired twin girl-brides it seemed impossible not to think that he was somehow plugged into their vital forces, in some mznner draining off energy before it could reach the women to power their thin, narrow feet, their stopped backs, their limp hair, their lacklustre eyes.

Uncle Sidney, possessed by this thought, laughed heartily into the room.

'What the hell are you laughing at, Sidney?' demanded James Henry.

Uncle Sidney shook his head and stopped.

James Henry glared at him. 'What was so funny, then?'

'Never mind,' said Uncle Sidney. 'It's enough to be able to laugh at all, the way things are.'

Then keep laughing, Sidney,' said James Henry. 'Keep at it, chum. You'll be fucking crying soon enough.'

Sidney grinned. 'So much for the good old values. Didn't you know there were ladies present?'

'What d'you mean?'

'Well, when I was a young man, we didn't use that sort of language in front of ladies.'

'What sort of language, you old fool?'

'You said "fucking", James,' said Uncle Sidney, straight-faced.

'Of course I didn't. I don't believe in . . . A man has to have a very limited vocabulary if he needs to resort to swearing like that. What are you trying to prove, Sidney?'

Again the look of vague astonishment crept into Uncle Sidney's eyes. 'Forget it,' he said at length.

'Are you trying to start something?'

'I don't want to start anything more, no,' said Uncle Sidney.

The television screen jumped from one scene to another. Fires and riots. Riots and fires.

James Henry turned to his wives. 'Did I say anything objectionable?'

In unison they shook their heads.

He glared again at Uncle Sidney. 'There you are!'

'Okay. All right.' Uncle Sidney looked away.

'I proved I didn't say anything,' said James Henry insistently.

'Fair enough.'

'They're my witnesses!' He pointed back at his wives. 'They told you.'

'Sure.'

'What do you mean — "sure"?'

'I meant I believe you. I'm sorry. I must have misheard you.'

James Henry relaxed and smiled. 'You might apologise, then. To all of us, I should have thought.'

'I apologise to all of you,' Uncle Sidney said. 'All of you.'

Ryan watched from the doorway and he was frowning. He looked at Uncle Sidney. He looked at James Henry. He looked at Ida and Felicity. He looked at Fred Masterson. Then he looked at the television screen.

It was not so different. It was frightening. Nothing seemed real. Or perhaps it was that nothing seemed any more real than anything else.

He went towards the television with the intention of switching it off. Then he paused. He was overwhelmed with the feeling that if he turned the switch not just the television picture would fade, but also the scene in the room. He shuddered.

Mr Ryan shuddered, full of fear and hopelessness. Full of depression. Full of doubt.

It had been a bad day.

The day was really something of an historic day, he thought. Today marked the turning point in his country's history — perhaps the world's history.

Perhaps it was the beginning of a new Dark Age.

He came to a decision and reached forward to switch off . . .

CHAPTER SIX

Seated in his little cabin, the television flickering gently in front of him, the foreign voices speaking their lines, Ryan falls, against his will, into a doze.

Surely he knew, when he sat down, when he selected a film in an alien language, that this would be the result. Perhaps he did but would not acknowledge the thought.

Ryan, a man tormented by nightmares during his official hours of sleep, who rises every morning with the indefinable despair of a man who has dreamed of horrors he cannot even remember — Ryan is desperate for rest.

Through the caverns of his brain pound the sounds of heart and blood, the drums of life. He hears them dimly at first.

Ryan is standing in the ballroom.
　The dance floor has a dull shine.
　　The lights in the candelabra are low.
　　　They give off a bluish light.
　　Black streamers decorate the walls.
　There are masks suspended at eye level on them.
The masks show human faces.

```
              K
               E
                E
                 P
                   GOING
                 P
                E
               E
              K
```

　　　The spaceship is on course for Munich. Travelling at just
below the speed of light.
　　　The spaceship is on course for Munich.

　　　I KNOW THAT I DES ...
... DES SCIENCES — HISTOIRE DES SCIENCES — HIS-
TOIRE DES SCIENCES ...

　　　IT IS TRUE, HOWEVER
　　　I AM WILLING TO TELL
　　　WHOEVER WISHES TO KNOW

(*there is no need to tell — there is no one to tell — it does not
matter ...*)

```
        K
       E
      E
     P
GOING
     P
      E
       E
        K
```

　　　　　WHICH WAY?
　　　　　　　*

In the ballroom the masks show human faces. Faces distorted by anger, lust and greed.

Suddenly one of the masks shows his wife Josephine, her face ferociously distorted. There is his youngest child, Alexander. His mouth is open, his eyes are blank. Alexander — a drooling idiot.

The couples are circling to the chanting music. It grows slower and slower and they revolve slower and slower. They are dressed in dark clothes. They have the firm and well-defined faces of the practical, self-interested, well-fed middle classes. They are people of substance.

Their eyes are masked by the round sun-glasses. The long closed windows at the end of the room look out into blackness. The music gets slower, the men and women revolve more slowly, so slowly they barely move at all.

The music almost stops.

There is a slow beating of a drum.

The music is heard more loudly. It is like a psalm sung by a chorus of monks. It is a funeral dirge, the song sung when a man is about to be buried.

The drums beat louder, the music quickens.

A high screaming note comes in and holds steady through the dirge.

The drum beats faster, the music quickens.

The high screams grow louder.

The dancers bunch in the middle of the room, staring towards the window through their round, black, covered eyes. They begin to talk quietly among themselves. They are discussing something and looking at the window.

*

ON THE NIGHT OF THE FAIR THERE WAS AN ACCI-
DENT.
  Q: WHAT WAS THE EXACT NATURE OF THE
  CATASTROPHE?
ON THE NIGHT OF THE MARINOS AN ACCIDENT
  Q: WHAT WAS THE EXACT NATURE OF THE
  CATASTROPHE?
ON A NIGHT IN MAY AN ACCIDENT
  Q: WHAT WAS THE EXACT NATURE OF THE
  CATASTROPHE?
ON AND ON MAY ACCIDENT
  Q: WHAT WAS THE EXACT NATURE OF THE
  CATASTROPHE?

ONE MAY ACCIDENT.
  Q: WHAT WAS THE EXACT NATURE OF THE
  CATASTROPHE?
ONE MAY ACCEPT
  Q: WHAT WAS THE EXACT NATURE OF THE
  CATASTROPHE?
ONE MACE IT
  Q: WHAT WAS THE EXACT NATURE OF THE
  CATASTROPHE?
ONE ACED
  Q: WHAT WAS THE EXACT NATURE OF THE
  CATASTROPHE?
ONE A
  Q: WHAT WAS THE EXACT NATURE OF THE
  CATASTROPHE?
ONE
  Q: WHAT WAS THE EXACT NATURE OF THE
  CATASTROPHE?
WON
  Q: WHAT WAS THE EXACT NATURE OF THE
  CATASTROPHE?
WIN
  Q: WHAT WAS THE EXACT NATURE OF THE
  CATASTROPHE?
IN
  Q: WHAT WAS THE EXACT NATURE OF THE
  CATASTROPHE?
N
  Q: WHAT WAS THE EXACT NATURE OF THE
  CATASTROPHE?
NO ANSWER AVAILABLE
NO ANSWER AVAILABLE
NO ANSWER AVAILABLE
END OF SESSION. PLEASE CLEAR ALL PREVIOUS
JUNK AND RESET IF REQUIRED.

*

They are still looking at the window.

Ryan finds himself and his wife and their two children standing in front of the window. His arm is around Josephine on one side and his other arm spans the shoulders of the two boys on the other.

The crowd is talking about them. Ryan feels fear for his wife and children. The crowd talks more angrily, looks at Ryan and his family.

The scream behind the music is louder, the singing more urgent, the drum beats faster, faster, faster.

*

THE SPACESHIP IS ON COURSE FOR MUNICH.
ON COURSE   TRAVELLING AT JUST BELOW THE SPEED OF LIGHT.
THE SPACESHIP IS ON COURSE FOR MUNICH.

*

CONDITION STEADY
CONDITION STEADY
CONDITION STEADY

The light flashes on and off as if trying to warn him of something rather than to reassure him. He frowns at the big sign. Is there something wrong with the hibernating personnel. Something he has not noticed? Something the instruments have not registered?

*

And Ryan awakes sweating in his red, inflatable chair and stares blindly at the minute, flat figures on the television screen.

His body is limp and his mouth is dry.

He licks his lips and sighs aloud.

Then he sets his mouth in a firm line, switches off the set and leaves the room.

His feet echo along the passageway. He reaches a cubicle containing a long white bed. He straps himself on and is massaged.

When he is finished his body aches and his mind is still not clear. It is now time for Ryan to eat. He returns to his room and gets food. He eats and he tastes nothing.

When he has finished he raises the cover over the porthole screen in his room and looks out through the simulated window into the vastness of space.

For a second he feels that he sees a dark figure out there in the void. He clears his vision rapidly and stares out at the stars.

He cannot see the planet that he and his companions are bound for. He has been in space for three years. He will be in space for another two years. And he cannot see his destination yet. He has only the word of the space physicists that it exists and that it can support the thirteen lives he carries with him. A planet of Barnard's

He is alone in space, in charge of his ship and the lives of the other twelve. He is more than halfway to his destination.

The sudden remembrance of what he has done sweeps over him. Along with his fear, with the torment caused by the solitude, Ryan feels pride. He causes the cover to sweep down over the 'porthole'. He leaves his room and walks into the control room to continue his duties.

But he cannot get rid of the lingering feeling of depression, the sense of something not done.

This sense of a task unfulfilled makes him work with even greater intensity, even greater efficiency.

He frowns.

There is still something left undone.

He rechecks everything. He runs tests through the computer. He inspects every instrument and double-checks it to make sure it is reading accurately.

Everything is perfect.

He has forgotten nothing.

The feeling almost disappears.

CHAPTER SEVEN

When he has read his report into the machine Ryan goes to the desk beneath the screen and opens the drawer where his red log-book is lying ready for his remarks.

First he sits down at his desk and hums a song as he completes some calculations. He works quickly and mechanically to complete his task. He lays it aside, satisfied.

He has fifteen minutes free now. He produces the red log-book from the drawer again, rules a line under his formal report and writes:

Alone in the craft I experience the heights and depths of emotion untempered by the needs of less mechanical work than I do now, uninterrupted by the presence of others.

He reads this over, frowns, shrugs, continues:

This means deep pain and being a prey to my own feelings. It also means great joy. An hour ago I stared out of my porthole at the enormous vista and recollected what I — what we as a group — have done to save ourselves. My mind goes back to how we were, and forward to what we will be.

Ryan's stylus hovers over the page. He makes writing motions over the book, but he cannot phrase his thoughts.

At length he gives up, rules another line under his entry, shuts the book and replaces it in the drawer.

He changes his mind, gets the book out again and begins to write rapidly:

The world was sick and even our group was tinged with unhealthiness. We were not lilywhite. We sold out some of our ideals. But perhaps the difference was that we knew we were selling out. We admitted what we were doing and so remained rational when almost everyone else had gone insane.

It is true, too, that we became somewhat hardened to the horrors around us, shut them out — even condoned some of them — even fell in with the herd from time to time. But we had our objectives — our sense of purpose. It kept us going. However, I don't deny that we dirtied our hands sometimes. I don't deny that I got carried away sometimes and did things that I now am inclined to regret. But perhaps it was worth it. After all, we survived!

Perhaps that is all the justification needed.

We kept our heads and we are now on our way to colonise a new planet. Start a new society on cleaner, more decent, more rational lines.

Cynics might think that an impossible ideal. It will all get just as bad in time, they'd say. Well, maybe it won't. Maybe this time we really can build a sane society!

None of us is perfect. Especially this crew! We all have our rows and we all have qualities that the others find annoying. But the point is that we are a family. Being a family, we can have our arguments, our strong disagreements — even our hatreds, to a degree — and still survive.

That is our strength.

Ryan yawns and checks the time. He still has a few minutes free time to spare. He looks at the paper and begins to write again:

When I look back to our days on Earth, particularly towards the end, I realise just how tense we were. The ship routine has relaxed me, allowed me to realise just what I had become. I don't like what I became. Perhaps one has to become a wolf, however, to fight wolves. It will never happen again. There were times, I cannot deny, when I lost hold of my ideals — even my senses. Some of the events are hazy — some are almost completely forgotten (though doubtless one of my relatives or friends will be able to remind me). I can hardly believe that it took such a short time for society to collapse.

That was what caused the trauma, of course — the suddenness of it all. Obviously, there were signs of the coming crises, and perhaps I should have taken more heed of those signs — but then all chaos suddenly broke loose throughout the world! What we tut-tutted at in the manner of older people slightly disconcerted by the changing times I now realise were much more serious indications of social unrest. Sudden increases in population, decreases in food production — they were the old problems that the Jeremiah had been going on about for years — but they were suddenly with us. Perhaps we had been deliberately refusing to face the problem, just as people had refused to consider the possibility of war with Germany in the late thirties. We homo sapiens have a great capacity for burying our heads in the sand while pretending to face out the issues.

Ryan smiles grimly. It's true, he thinks. People under stress usually start dealing with half a dozen surrogate issues, leaving the real issues completely untouched because they're too difficult to cope with. Like the man who lost the sixpence in the house but decided to look for it outside because the light was better and he would thus save his candles.

He adds in his log:

And there's always some bloody messiah to answer their needs — someone whom they will follow blindly because they are too fearful to rely on their own good sense. It's like Don Quixote leading the Gadarene Swine!

Ryan chuckles aloud.

Leaders, fuhrers, duces, prophets, visionaries, gurus . . . For a hundred years the world was ruled by bad poets. A good politician is only something of a visionary—essentially he must be a man who sees the needs of people in practical and immediate terms and tries to do something about it. Visionaries are fine for inspiring people — but they are the worst choice as leaders — they attempt to impose their rather simple visions on an extremely complicated world! Why have politics and art become so mixed up together in the last hundred years? Why have bad artists been given nations as canvases on which to paint their tatty, sketchy, rubbish? Perhaps because politics, like religion before it, was dead as an effective force and something new had to be found. And art stood in until whatever it was turned up. Will something turn up? It's hard to say. We'll probably never know on Munich 15040 if the world survives or not.

Thank God we had the initiative to get this ship on her way to the stars!

No more time for writing. Ryan puts the log-book away quickly and begins his regular check of the ship's nuclear drive, running a check on virtually every separate component.

He taught himself the procedure for running the ship. He was not trained as an astronaut. No one planned that he should be the man standing in the control cabin at that particular moment.

Until comparatively recently Ryan was, in fact, a business man. A pretty successful business man.

As he does the routine checking, he thinks about himself before he even conceived the idea of travelling into space.

He sees himself, a strongly built man of forty, standing with his back to the vast plate glass window of his large, thickly carpeted office. His heavy, healthy face was pugnacious, his back was broad, his thick, stubby-fingered hands were clasped behind his back.

Where Ryan is now a monk — a man dedicated to his ship and his unconscious companions — a man charged, like a cleric in the Dark Ages, with preserving the knowledge and lives contained in this moving monastery — then he was a man almost perpetually in a state of combat.

Ten thousand years before he would have been a savage standing in front of his pack, hair bristling, teeth bared, bone club in hand.

Instead, Ryan had been a toymaker.

Not a kindly old peasant whittling puppets in a pretty little cottage. Ryan had owned a firm averaging a million pounds a year in profits, producing toy videophones, plastic hammers, miniature miracles of rocketry, talking life-size dolls, knee-high cars with automatic gear changes, genuine all electric cooking machines, real baaing sheep, things which jumped, sped, made noises and broke when their calculated life-span was over and were thrown secretly and with curses by parents into the rapid waste disposal units of cities all over the western world.

Ryan pressed the button which connected him with the office of his manager, Owen Powell.

Powell appeared on the screen. He was on his hands and knees on the office floor watching two dolls, three foot high, walk about the carpet. As he heard the buzz of the interoffice communicator he was saying to one of the dolls: 'Hello, Gwendolen.' As he said 'Hello, Ryan,' the doll replied, in a beautifully modulated voice, 'Hello, Owen.'

'That's the personalised doll you were talking about, is it?' Ryan said.

'That's it.' Powell straightened up. 'I knew they could do it if they tried. Lovely, isn't she? The child voice-prints her in the shop on its birthday, say. After that she can give any one of twenty five responses to its questions — but only to the child. Imagine that — a doll which can speak, apparently intelligently, *but only to you.* The kids go mad about it.'

'If the price is right,' Ryan said.

Powell was an enthusiast, a man who would really, if he had not had a twenty thousand pound a year job with Ryan, have been perfectly happy carving toys in an old peasant's hut. He looked disconcerted by Ryan's discouraging remark.

'Well, maybe we can get the price down to twenty pounds retail. What would you say to that?'

'Not bad.' Ryan deliberately gave Powell no encouragement. Powell was a man who would work hard for a smile and stop working when you gave it, reasoned Ryan. Therefore it was better to smile seldom in his direction.

'Never mind all that now.' Ryan rubbed his eyebrows. 'There's plenty of time to get it right before Christmas when we'll try a few out, see how they go and produce a big line by spring for the following Christmas.'

Powell nodded. 'Agreed.'

'Now,' said Ryan, 'I want you to do two things for me. One — get in touch with the factory and tell Ames to use the Mark IV pin on the Queen of Dolls. Two — ring Davies and tell him we're stopping all deliveries until he pays.'

'He'll never keep going during August if we do that,' objected Powell. 'If we stop delivering, he'll have to close down, man. We'll only get a fraction of what he owes us!'

'I don't care.' Ryan gestured dismissively. 'I'm not letting Davies get away with another ten thousand pounds worth of goods so that he'll pay us in the end, if we're lucky. I will not do business on that basis, That's final.'

'All right.' Powell shrugged. 'That's reasonable enough.'

'I think so.' Ryan broke the connection.

He reached into his desk and took out a bottle of green pills. He poured water into a glass from an old-fashioned carafe on his immaculate desk. He swallowed the pills and put the glass down. Unconsciously he resumed his stance, head jutting slightly forward, hands behind back. He had a decision to make.

Powell was a good manager.

A bit sloppy sometimes. Forgetful. But on the whole efficient. He was not quarrelsome, like the ambitious Conroy, or withdrawn, like his last manager, Evers.

What he had mistaken at first for decent behaviour, respect for another man's privacy, had gone beyond reason in Evers.

When a manager refused to speak to the firm's managing director on the interoffice communicator — broke the connection consistently in fact — business became impossible.

Ryan could certainly respect his feelings, sympathize with them as it happened — so would any other self-respecting person. But facts were facts. You could not run a business without talking to other people. Strangers they might be, uncongenial they might be, but if you couldn't stand a brief conversation on the communicator, then you were no use to a firm.

Ryan reflected that he himself was finding it increasingly distasteful to get in touch with many of his key workers but, since it was that or go under, he forced himself to do so.

Powell was certainly a good manager.

Inventive and clever, too.

On the other hand, Ryan thought, he had come to hate him.

He was — childish. There was no other word for it. That open countenance, that smile, a smile which said that he would take to anybody who took to him. There was something doglike about it. Just pat him on the head and he would wag his tail to and fro, jump up and lick your face. Sickening, really, Ryan thought to himself. It made you feel sick to think about it. He had no reticences, no reserves. A man shouldn't be so friendly.

And, of course, Ryan thought, when you looked at the facts, it all came down to Powell's being Welsh. That was the Welshman for you — openfaced and friendly when they spoke to you and clannishly against you behind your back.

The Welsh gangs were some of the worst in the city. Ryan reflected that he had not bought his machine gun, and taught his wife and elder son how to use it, just for fun. That was the Welsh — all handshakes and smiles when you met them, and all the time their sons were stoning your relatives three streets away.

Ryan tapped his teeth together. Old Saunders of Happyvoice had shaken him a bit when he had got on the communicator just to warn him about Powell.

'It might help,' he had said, 'if that manager of yours, Powell, changed his name. You can't deny it sounds Welsh and there's been an awful lot of trouble with those Welsh Nationalists recently. Between ourselves, it only needs one word from a competitor of yours — say Moonbeam Toys — via their PRO, and you'll be branded in the press as an employer of Welsh labour. And that's never likely to help sales — because people remember. Just at that critical moment when they're choosing between one of your products and one of another firm's — they remember. And then they don't buy a Ryan Toy. See what I mean? One word from you to old Powell and he'll change his name to Smith and you're in the clear.'

Ryan had smiled bluffly and made assurances. When he had cut off the communicator two thoughts came to him.

One, he knew Powell would be first confused and then obstinate about changing his name.

Two, and worse, that Saunders did not think for one instant that Powell was a Welshman. He just thought he had an unfortunate name.

Ryan realised that he was right out on a limb. Where his competitors refused to take on employees with suspect names, however impeccable their backgrounds, Ryan had an actual living, breathing Welshman working for him. Someone who could quite easily be a Nationalist, working for the Welsh Cause (a somewhat obscure Cause as Ryan saw it). It was bloody ridiculous. How could he have got so out of touch? Why hadn't he thought of it?

Ryan frowned. No — it was stupid. Powell was too absorbed in his work to worry about politics. He was the last person to get involved in anything like that.

Still, a name was a name. The Nationalists had been causing quite a bit of trouble lately and things had really got bad with the assassination of the King. The Welsh Nationalists had claimed it was their work. But other groups of extremists had also made the same claim.

From a practical point of view, Ryan thought, Powell was an embarrassment. No question of it. Yet he couldn't fire a man on suspicion.

Ryan's face took on an over-rosy tinge and his thick hands gripped each other a little more firmly behind his back.

I'm in fucking trouble here, he thought.

He pinched his nose and then reached out to buzz for his personnel manager.

Frederick Masterson was sitting at his desk working on a graph. Masterson was, in physical terms, the exact complement to Ryan. Where Ryan was thickset and ruddy, Masterson was tall, thin and pale. As the communicator buzzed in his office he dropped the pencil from his long, thin hand and looked at the screen in alarm. Seeing Ryan, a thin smile came to his lips.

'Oh, it's you,' he said.

'Fred. I want details of any staff we employ with foreign or strange-sounding names — or foreign backgrounds of any kind. Just to be on the safe side, you realise. I'm not planning a purge!' He laughed briefly.

'Just as well,' Masterson grinned. 'Your name's Irish isn't it, begorrah!'

Ryan said: 'Come off it, Fred. I'm no more Irish than you are. Not a single relative or ancestor for the past hundred years has even seen Ireland, let alone come from it.'

'I know, I know,' said Fred. 'Call me Oirish agin and Oi'll knock ye over the hade wid me shillelegh.'

'Skip the funny imitations, Fred,' Ryan said shortly. 'The firm's at stake. You know how bloody small-minded a lot of people are. Well it seems to be getting worse. I just don't want to take any chances. I want you to probe. If necessary turn the whole department over to examining personnel records for the slightest hint of anything peculiar. Examine marriages, family background, schooling, previous places of employment. No action at this stage. I'm not planning to victimise anyone.'

'Not at the moment,' said Masterson, a funny note in his voice.

'Oh, come off it, Fred. I just want to be prepared. In case any competitors start going for us. Naturally I'll protect my employees to the hilt. This is one way of making sure I can protect them — against any scandal, for a start.'

Masterson sighed. 'What about those with Negro blood? I mean the West Indians got around a bit before they were all sent back.'

'Okay. I don't think anyone's got anything against blacks at the moment have they?'

'Not at the moment.'

'Fine.'

'But you never know . . .'

'No.'

'I want to protect them, Fred.'

'Of course.'

Ryan cut the communicator and sighed.

An image flashed into his mind and with a start he remembered a dream he had had the previous night. It was funny, the way you suddenly remembered dreams long after you had dreamt them.

It had been to do with a cat. His old house where he had lived with his parents. It had had a big, overgrown back garden and they had kept several cats. The dream was to do with the air rifle he had had and a white and ginger cat — an interloper — that had entered the garden. Someone — not himself, as he remembered the dream

— had shot the cat. He had not wanted to shoot the cat himself, but had gone along with this other person. They had shot the cat once and it had been patched up by neighbours. There had been a piece of sticking plaster on its left flank. The person had fired the gun and badly wounded the cat but the animal had not appeared to notice. It had still come confidently along the wall, tail up and purring, towards the French windows. It had had a big, bloody wound in its side, but it hadn't seemed to be aware of it.

The cat had entered the house and come into the kitchen, still purring, and eaten from the bowl of one of the resident cats.

Ryan had not known whether to kill it to put it out of its misery or whether to let it be. It hadn't actually seemed to be in any misery, that was the strange thing.

Ryan shook his head. A disturbing dream. Why should he remember it now?

He had never, after all, owned a white and ginger cat.

Ryan shrugged. Good God, this was no time for worrying about silly dreams. He would have to do some hard thinking. Some realistic thinking. He prided himself that if he was nothing else he was a pragmatist. Not an ogre. He was well-known for his good qualities as an employer. He had the best staff in the toy industry. People were only too eager to come and work for Ryan Toys. The pay was better. The conditions were better. Ryan was much respected by his fellow employers and by the trades unions. There had never been any trouble at Ryan Toys.

But he had the business to consider. And, of course, ultimately the country, for Ryan's exports were high.

Or had been, thought Ryan, before the massive wave of nationalism had swept the world and all but frozen trade, save for the basic necessities.

Still, it would pass. A bit of a shake-up for everybody. It wasn't a bad thing. Made people keep their feet on the ground. One had to know how to ride these peculiar political crises that came and went. He wasn't particularly politically minded himself. A liberal with a small *l* was how he liked to describe himself. He had an excellent profit-sharing scheme in the factory, lots of fringe benefits, and an agreement with the unions that on his death the workers would take over control of the factory, paying a certain percentage of profits to his dependants. He was all for socialism so long as it was phased in painlessly. He steadfastly refused to have a private doctor and took his chances with the National Health Service along with everybody else. While he was not over-friendly with his workers, he was on good terms with them and they liked

43

him. This silly racialistic stuff would come and go.

The odds were that it wouldn't affect the factory at all.

Ryan took a deep breath. He was getting over-anxious, that was his trouble. Probably that bloody Davies account preying on his mind. It was just as well to take a stiff line with Davies, even if it meant losing a few thousand. He would rather kiss the money goodbye if it meant kissing goodbye to the worries that went with it.

He buzzed through to Powell again.

Powell was once again on his knees, fiddling with a doll.

'Ah,' said Powell straightening up.

'Did you take care of those couple of items, Powell?'

'Yes. I spoke to Ames and I phoned Davies. He said he'd do his best.'

'Good man,' Ryan said and switched off hastily as a delighted grin spread over Powell's face.

CHAPTER EIGHT

Ryan is working on a small problem that has come up concerning the liquid regeneration unit in the forward part of the ship. It is malfunctioning slightly and the water has a slight taste of urine in it. A spare part is needed and he is instructing the little servorobot to replace the defunct element.

That was what had saved him, of course, he thought. His pragmatism. He had kept his head while all around people were losing theirs, getting hysterical, making stupid decisions — or worse, making no decisions at all.

He smiles. He had always made quick decisions. Even when those decisions were unpalatable or possibly unfashionable in terms of the current thinking of the time. It was his basic hardheadedness that had kept him going longer than most of them, allowed him to hang on to a lot more, helped him to the point where he was now safely out of the mess that was the disrupted, insane society of Earth.

And that is how he intends to remain. He must keep cool, not let the depression, the aching loneliness, the weaker elements of his character, take him over.

'I'll make it,' he murmurs confidently to himself. 'I'll make it. Those people are going to get their chance to start all over again.'

He yawns. The muscles at the back of his neck are aching. He wriggles his shoulders, hoping to limber the muscles up. But the ache remains. He'll have to do something about that. Must stay fit at all costs. Not just himself to think of.

He isn't proud of everything he did on Earth. Some of those decisions would not have been made under different circumstances.

But he didn't go mad.

Not the way so many of the others did.

He stayed sane. Just barely, sometimes, but he made it through to the other side. He kept his eyes clear and saw things as they really were while a lot of other people were chasing wild geese or phantom tigers. It was a struggle, naturally. And sometimes he had made mistakes. But his common sense hadn't let him down — not in the long run.

What had someone once said to him?

He nodded to himself. That was it. *You're a survivor, Ryan. A natural bloody survivor.*

It was truer now, of course, than ever before.

He was a survivor. *The* survivor. He and his friends and relatives.

He was making for the clean, fresh world untainted by mankind, leaving the rest of them to rot in the shit heap they had created.

Yet he mustn't feel proud. Pride goeth before a fall . . . Mustn't get egocentric. There had been a good deal of luck involved. It wasn't such a bad idea to test himself from time to time, run through that Old Time Religion stuff. The seven deadly sins.

Check his own psyche out the way he checked the ship.

CHECK FOR *PRIDE*.

CHECK FOR *ENVY*.

CHECK FOR *SLOTH*.

CHECK FOR *GLUTTONY*.

. . . and so forth. It didn't do any harm. It kept him sane. And he didn't reject the possibility that he *could* go insane. There was always a chance. He had to watch for the signs. Check them in time. A stitch in time saves nine.

That was how he had always operated.

And he hadn't done badly, after all.

REPAIR COMPLETED reports the computer. Ryan is satisfied.

'Congratulations,' he says cheerfully. 'Keep up the good work, chum.'

The point was, he thinks, that he, unlike so many of the rest, had never been to a psychiatrist in his life. He'd been his own psychiatrist. *Gluttony*, for instance, could indicate some kind of disturbance that came out in obsessive eating. Therefore if he found himself overeating, he searched for a reason, hunted out the cause of the problem. It was the same with work. If it started to get on top of you, then stop — take a holiday. It meant you could work better when you got back and didn't spend all your time bawling out your staff for mistakes that were essentially your own creation.

He presses a faucet button and samples the water. He smacks his lips. It's fine.

He is relaxing. The disturbing dreams, the sense of depression have been replaced by a feeling of well-being. He has compensated in time. Instead of looking back at the bad times, he is looking back at the good times. That is how it should be.

CHAPTER NINE

Masterson flashed Ryan about a week after he had begun his check-up.

Ryan had been feeling good for days. The Davies matter was settled. Davies had paid up two-thirds of the amount and they had called it quits. To show no hard feelings Ryan had even paid off the mortgage on Davies' apartment so that he would have somewhere secure to live after he had sold up his business.

'Morning, Fred. What's new?'

'I've been doing that work you asked for.'

'Any results?'

'I think all the results are in. I've drawn up a graph of our findings on the subject.'

'How does the graph look?'

'It'll come as a shock to you.' Masterson pursed his lips. 'I think I'd better come and talk to you personally. Show you the stuff I've got. Okay?'

'Well — of course — yes. Okay, Fred. When do you want to come here?'

'Right away?'

'Give me half an hour.'

'Fine.'

Ryan used the half hour to prepare himself for Masterson's visit, tidying his desk, putting everything away that could be put away, straightening the chairs.

When Masterson arrived he was sitting at his desk smiling.

Masterson spread out the graph.

'I see what you mean,' said Ryan. 'Good heavens! Just as well we decided to do this, eh?'

'It confirms what I already believed,' said Masterson. 'Ten per cent of your employees, chiefly from the factories in the North, are actually of wholly foreign parentage — Australian and Irish in the main. Another ten per cent had parents born outside England itself, i.e. in Scotland, Wales and the Republic of Ireland. Three per cent of your staff, although born and educated in England, are Jewish. About half a per cent have Negro or Asiatic blood. That's the general picture.'

Ryan rubbed his nose. 'Bloody difficult, eh, Masterson?'

Masterson shrugged. 'It could be used against us. There are a number of ways. If the government offers tax relief to firms employing one hundred per cent English labour, as they're talking of doing, then we aren't going to benefit from the tax relief. Then there are wholesaler's and retailer's embargos if our rivals release this information. Lastly there's the customers.'

Ryan licked his lips thoughtfully. 'It's a tricky one, Fred.'

'Yes. Tricky.'

'Oh, fuck, Fred.' Ryan scratched his head. 'There's only one assumption, isn't there?'

'If you want to survive,' said Fred, 'yes.'

'It means sacrificing a few in order to protect the many. We'll pay them generous severance pay, of course.'

'It's something like thirty-five per cent of your employees.'

'We'll phase them out gradually, of course.' Ryan sighed. 'I'll have to have a talk with the unions. I don't think they'll give us any trouble. They'll see the sense of it. They always have.'

'Make sure of it,' said Masterson, 'first.'

'Naturally. What's up, Fred? You seem fed up about something.'

'Well, you know as well as I do what this means. You'll have to get rid of Powell, too.'

'He won't suffer from it. I'm not a bloody monster, Fred. You've got to adjust though. It's the only way to survive. We've got to be realistic. If I stood on some abstract ideal, the whole firm would collapse within six months. You know that. The one thing all political parties are agreed on is that many of our troubles stem

47

from an over-indulgent attitude towards foreign labour. Whichever way the wind blows in the near future, there's no escaping that one. And the way our rivals are fighting these days, we can't afford to go around wearing kid gloves and sniffing bloody daffodils.'

'I realise that,' said Masterson. 'Of course.'

'Powell won't feel a thing. He'd rather be running a doll's hospital or a toyshop, anyway. I'll do that. I'll buy him a bloody toyshop. What do you say? That way everybody's happy.'

'Okay,' said Masterson. 'Sounds a good idea.' He rolled up the charts. 'I'll leave the breakdown with you to go over.' He made for the door.

'Thanks a lot, Fred,' Ryan said gratefully. 'A lot of hard work. Very useful. Thanks.'

'It's my job,' said Masterson. 'Cheerio. Keep smiling.' He left the office.

Ryan was relieved that he had gone. He couldn't help the irrational feeling of invasion he had whenever anyone came into his office. He sat back, humming, and studied Masterson's figures.

You had to stay ahead of the game.

But Masterson had put his finger on the only real problem. He disliked the idea of firing Powell in spite of the man's unbearable friendliness, his nauseating candour, his stupid assumption that you only had to give one happy grin to open the great dam of smiles swirling about in everyone.

Ryan grinned in spite of himself. That summed up poor old Powell all right.

As a manager, as a creative man, Powell was first class. Ryan could think of no one in the business who could more than half fill his place. He wasn't any trouble. He was content. A willing worker putting in much longer hours than were expected of him.

But was that just his good-heartedness? Ryan wondered. A light was dawning. Now he could see it. Powell was probably just grateful to have a job! He knew that no one in any business would employ him.

Just like a bloody Welshman to hang on and on, not letting you know the facts, creeping about, getting good money out of you, not letting you know that his very presence was threatening to ruin your business. Trying to make himself indispensible in the hopes that you'd never find out about him and fire him. Pleasant and agreeable and co-operative. Maybe even a front for some sort of Welsh Nationalist sabotage. Then — the knife in the back, the bullet from the window, the enemy in the alley.

Stop it, Ryan told himself. Powell wasn't like that. He didn't need to build the man up into a villain to justify sacking him. There was only one reason for sacking him. He was an embarrassment. He could harm the firm.

Ryan relaxed.

He sat down at his desk, opened a drawer and took out his packed lunch. He opened the thermos flask and poured himself a cup of coffee. He placed his meal on the miniature heater in the lower compartment of the luncheon box.

Thank God, he thought, for the abolition of those communal lunches with other business men, or the firm's executives.

Thank God that communal eating had finally died the death. What could have been more disgusting than sitting munching and swallowing with a gang of total strangers, sitting there staring at their moving mouths, offering them items — wine, salt, pepper, water — to make their own consumption more palatable, talking to them face to face as they nourished themselves. The conversion of the canteens had provided much-needed office space as well.

Ryan took a fork and dug into the plate. The food was now thoroughly heated.

Once he had eaten he felt even more relaxed. He had thought it all out. He didn't waste time when it came to decisions. No point in moralising.

He wiped his lips.

The problem had assumed its proper proportions. It would cost him a bit in golden and silver handshakes, but it was worth it. He could probably get cheaper staff anyway, considering the huge volume of unemployment, and recoup his losses by the end of the year.

This way everybody gains something. Nobody lost.

He picked up the sheets of names and figures and began to study them closely.

CHAPTER TEN

That's how it was, thinks Ryan. A cop out, now he looked back, but a graceful cop out. No one got badly hurt. It could have been worse. It was the difference between a stupid approach and an intelligent approach to the same problem.

It had been the same when he had got the group out of that riot at the Patriot meeting. When had that been? January. Yes. January 2000. The civilised world had been expecting the end. There had been all the usual sort of apocalyptic stuff which Ryan had dismissed as a symptom of radical social change. He had not been able to believe then that things were going to get worse. There had been penitential marches through the streets. Even scourgings, public confessions.

And January had been the month of that oddball move to close the camps for foreigners. The camps had been decently maintained. The people lived as well as anyone outside the camps — perhaps better in certain circumstances. It had also been the month when the Patriots had tried to open the camps up to more people — to a more sinister, less identifiable group.

Ryan remembers the crowd in Trafalgar Square. A crowd fifty thousand strong, covering the square, pushed up the steps of the National Gallery and St Martin's, pushed inside the Gallery and the Church, right up against the altar. The crowd had blocked the streets all around. It was horrifying. Disgusting. People like rats in a box.

Even now Ryan feels sick, remembering how he felt then.

He and the group had gone along, but they were now regretting it.

Whenever the crowd got too noisy or violent the troops fired over their heads.

It had been snowing. The searchlights played over the plinth where the leading Patriots stood and they flashed over the heads of the crowd, picked up large flakes of snow as they drifted down on the dense mass of people.

The Patriot leaders, collars of their dark coats turned up, stood in the snow looking over the crowd. And as they spoke their voices were enormously amplified. Deafeningly amplified; reaching all the way up the Mall to where Queen Anne sat in her lonely room, hearing the words on TV and from the meeting itself a quarter of a mile away; reaching all the way down Whitehall to Parliament itself.

Parliament. That discredited institution.

They are turning on each other now, thought Ryan, looking at the faces of the Patriots. There were signs of dissension there if he wasn't mistaken. There would be a split soon.

But meanwhile there were the usual speeches, coming distorted into the mind partly because of the amplification system, partly because of the wind, partly because of the usual ungraspable

50

political clichés the speakers used.

The snow kept falling on the upturned faces of the crowd — an orderly crowd of responsible people. There were few interrupters. The presence of the troops and the paid Patriot Guards made sure of that.

Colin Beesley, Patriot leader and Member of Parliament, stood up to speak.

Beesley, a large, thickset man in a long, black overcoat and a large hat, was an extremist. His political manner was of the old school — the Churchillian school which still touched many people who wanted their politicians to be 'strong'. His tone was ponderous. His words, spoken slowly and relatively clearly, were portentous.

Unlike the others, he did not speak generally about the Patriot cause, for he had come to make a fresh statement.

As he began to speak the wind dropped and his words came through with a sudden clarity — over the crowd in the square, the crowds in the streets, down as far as Westminster, along to Buckingham Palace, as far as Piccadilly Circus in the other direction.

'Aliens among us,' he said, his head lowered and thrust towards the crowd. 'There are aliens among us. We do not know where they come from. We do not know how they landed. We do not know how many there are. But we do know one thing, my friends, people of England — they are among us!'

Ryan, standing uncomfortably in the middle of the crowd in the square grimaced sceptically at his friend Masterson who stood beside him. Ryan couldn't believe in a group of aliens contriving to land on Earth without anyone's knowledge. Not when the skies were scanned for invaders from special observation posts built all over the country. But Masterson was listening seriously and intently to Beesley.

Ryan turned his attention back to the platform.

'We cannot tell who they are, yet they are among us.' Beesley's voice droned on. 'They look like us, sound like us — in every respect they are human — but they are not human. They are non-human — they are anti-human.' He paused, lowered his voice. 'How, you say, do we know about the aliens? How have we found out about the existence of this pollution, of these creatures who move about our society, like cancer cells in a healthy body? We know, by the evidence of our own eyes. We know the aliens exist because of who they are, what happens when they are about.

'Otherwise how can we explain the existence of chaos, blood-

51

lust, law-breaking, riot, revolution in our midst? How can we explain the deaths of the little children battered to death by the fanatics of Yorkshire? The waves of rioting and looting all over the West Country? The satanic practices of religious maniacs in the Fens? How can we explain the hatred and the suspicion, the murder rate — now three times what it was five years ago, a full ten times what it was in 1990? How can we explain the fact that we have so few children when a few years ago the birth rate had doubled? Disaster is upon us! Who is stirring up and fomenting all this disorder, bloodshed and ruin. Who? Who?'

Ryan, glancing into the faces of the people about him, could almost believe they were listening seriously. Were they? Or was the presence of the troops and the Patriot Guards preventing them from catcalling or just walking away from this nonsense?

He looked at the faces of the police around the platform. They were staring up at Beesley — brute-faced men listening to him with close attention. Ryan, scarcely able to believe it, realised that Beesley's stories of the hidden invaders was being taken seriously by the majority of the vast crowd. As Beesley went on speaking, describing the hidden marauders, makers of chaos in their midst, the crowd began to murmur in agreement.

'Their bases are somewhere,' Beesley went on. 'We must find them, fellow patriots. We must eliminate them, like wasp nests . . .'

And there came from the crowd a great hissed susurrus 'Yesssss.'

'We must find the polluters and wipe them out forever. Whether they come from space or are the agents of another Power, we do not know as yet. We must discover where they originate!'

And the crowd like a cold wind through the ruins, answered 'Yessssss.'

He's lost them, thought Ryan sceptically, if he doesn't give them something a bit more concrete than that. He's got to tell them how to pick out these menacing figures they have to destroy.

'Who are they? How do we find them?' asked Beesley. 'How? How? How indeed?' His tone became divinely reasonable. 'You all know, in your heart of hearts, who they are. They are the men — and women, too, make no mistake, they are women as well — who are different. You know them. You can tell them at a glance. They look different. Their eyes are different. They express doubt where you and I know certainty. They are the men who associate with strangers and people of doubtful character, the men and women who throw suspicion on what we are fighting for. They are the sceptics, the heretics, the mockers. When you meet them they make you doubt everything, even yourself. They laugh a lot, and smile too often. They attempt, by jesting, to throw a poor light on our ideals. They are the people who hang back when plans are suggested for purifying our land. They defend the objects of our patriotic anger. They hang back from duty. Many are drunkards, licentious scoffers. You know these people, friends. You know them — these men who have been sent here to undermine a righteous society. You have always known them. Now is the time to pluck them out and deal with them as they deserve.'

And, before he had finished speaking, the crowd was in uproar. There were shouts and screams.

Ryan poked Masterson, who was staring incredulously at the platform, in the ribs. 'Let's get out,' he said. 'There's going to be trouble.'

'Only for the aliens,' said James Henry at his other elbow. 'Come on, Ryan. Let's sniff 'em out and snuff 'em out.'

Ryan looked at Henry in astonishment. Henry's green eyes were ablaze. 'For crying out loud, Henry . . .'

He turned to his brother John. John looked back vaguely and suddenly, under the gaze of his elder brother, seemed to pull himself together. 'He's right,' said John. 'We'd better think of getting home. This is real mass hysteria. Jesus Christ.'

Henry's mouth hardened. 'I'm staying.'

'Look —— ' Ryan was jolted by the crowd. Snow fell down his neck. ' — Henry! You can't possibly . . .'

'Do what you like, Ryan. We've heard the call to deal with these aliens — let's deal with them.'

'They wouldn't be likely to come here tonight would they?' Ryan shouted. Then he stopped, realising that he was beginning to answer in Henry's terms. That was the first step towards being convinced. 'Good God, Henry — this is too classic for words. We're rational men.'

'Agreed. Which makes our duty even clearer!'

The crowd was pushing the four men backwards and forwards. The men had to shout to be heard over the roar of the rabble.

'James — come home and talk it over. This isn't the place . . .' Ryan insisted, standing his ground with difficulty. From somewhere came the sound of gunfire. Then the gunfire stopped. Ryan found he was shouting into relative silence. 'You won't take that "aliens" nonsense seriously when you've got a drink inside you back at our flat!'

A man put his head over Henry's shoulder. His red face was

flushed. 'What was that, friend?' he said to Ryan.

'I wasn't talking to you.'

'Oh no? I heard what you said. That's of interest to *everyone* here. You're one of them, if you ask me.'

'I didn't.' Ryan looked contemptuously at the sweating face. 'But we're all entitled to our own opinions. If you think it's true, I won't argue with you.'

'Shut up,' Masterson cried, tugging at Ryan's sleeve. 'Shut up and come home.'

'Bloody alien!' the red-faced man shouted. 'A bloody nest of them!'

Instantly, it seemed to Ryan, the crowd was on them. He came rapidly to a decision, keeping his head even in this situation.

'Calm down all of you,' he said in his most commanding voice. 'My point is that we might make mistakes in this situation. The aliens have to be found. But we need to work systematically to find them. Use a scientific approach. Don't you see — the aliens themselves could be stirring things up for us — making us turn on each other.'

The red-faced man frowned. 'It's a point,' he said grudgingly.

'Now I believe that if there are aliens here tonight they are not going to be in the middle of the crowd. They are going to be on the edges, trying to sneak away,' Ryan continued.

'That seems reasonable,' said James Henry. 'Let's get after them.'

Ryan led the way shouting with the rest.

'Aliens! Aliens! Stop the aliens. Get them now. Over there — in the streets!'

Pushing through the crowd was like trying to trudge through a quagmire. Every step, every breath Ryan took was painful.

Ryan led them, pace by pace, through the packed throng, up the steps into the National Gallery and, as the crowd thinned out in the galleries themselves, through a window at the back, through yards, over walls and car parks until they escaped the red-faced man and his friends and were finally in the moving mass of Oxford Street.

Only James Henry didn't seem aware of what Ryan had done. As they reached Hyde Park he pulled at Ryan's torn coat.

'Hey! What are we supposed to be doing. I thought we were going after the aliens.'

'I know something about the aliens that wasn't mentioned tonight,' Ryan said.

'What?'

'I'll tell you when we get back to my place.'

When they finally reached Ryan's flat they were exhausted.

'What about the aliens, then?' James Henry asked as the door closed behind them.

'The worst aliens are the Patriots,' said Ryan. 'They are the most obvious of the anti-humans.'

Henry was puzzled. 'Surely not . . .'

Ryan took a deep breath and went to the drinks cabinet, began fixing drinks for them all as they sat panting in the chairs in the living room.

'The Patriots . . .' murmured Henry. 'I suppose it's just possible . . .'

Ryan handed him his drink. 'I thought,' he said, 'that the discoveries in Space would give us all a better perspective. Instead it seems that the perspective has been even more narrowed and distorted. Once people only feared other races, other nations, other groups with opposed or different interests. Now they fear everything. It's gone too far, Henry.'

'I'm still not with you,' James Henry said.

'Simply — paranoia. What is paranoia, Henry?'

'Being afraid of things — suspecting plots — all that stuff.'

'It can be defined more closely. It is an *irrational* fear, an *irrational* suspicion. Often it is in fact a refusal to face the *real* cause of one's anxiety, to invent causes because the true cause is either too disturbing, too frightening, too horrible to face or too difficult to cope with. That's what paranoia actually is, Henry.'

'So . . . ?'

'So the Patriots have offered us a surrogate. They have offered us something to concentrate on that is nothing really to do with the true causes of the ills of Society. It's common enough. Hitler supplied it to the Germans in the form of the Jews and the Bolsheviks. McCarthy supplied it to the Americans in the form of the Communist Conspiracy. Even our own Enoch Powell supplied it in the form of the West Indian immigrants in the sixties and seventies. There are plenty of examples.'

James Henry frowned. 'You say they were wrong, eh? Well, I'm not so sure. We were right to get rid of the West Indians when we did. We were right to restrict jobs to Englishmen when we did. You have to draw the line somewhere, Ryan.'

Ryan sighed. 'And what about these "aliens" from space, then? Where do they fit in? What are they doing to the economy? They are an invention — a crude invention, at that — of the Patriots to describe anyone who is opposed to their insane schemes. Where do you think the term "witch-hunt" comes from, Henry?'

James Henry sipped his drink thoughtfully. 'Perhaps I did get a bit over-excited . . .'

Ryan patted him on the shoulder. 'We all are. It's the strain, the tension — and it is particularly the uncertainty. We don't know where we're going. We've no goals, because we can't rely on Society any longer. The Patriots offer certainty. And that's what we've got to find for ourselves.'

'You'd better explain,' John Ryan said from his chair. 'Have you got any suggestions?'

Ryan spread his hands. 'That was my suggestion. That we find a goal — a rational goal. Find a way out of this mess . . .'

And Ryan, now sitting at his desk in the great ship, reflects that it was that evening which was the turning point, that decision which brought him to where he is now, aboard the spaceship *Hope Dempsey*, heading towards Munich 15040, Barnard's Star, at point nine of c . . .

CHAPTER ELEVEN

There is no sound here in space. No light. No life. Only the dim glow of distant stars as the tiny craft moves, so slowly, through the great neutral blackness.

And Ryan, as he goes methodically about his duties, thinks with a heavy heart of the familiarity and warmth of his early years — of the births of his children, of studying their first schoolbooks, talking to his friends in the evenings at their flat, of his wife, now resting like some comfortable Sleeping Beauty, unaware of him in the fluids of her casket.

Just a pellet travelling through space, thinks Ryan. Nearly all the living tissue contained in the pellet is unconscious in the waters of the caskets. Once they had moved and acted. They had been happy, until the threats had become obvious, until life had become unbearable for them . . .

Ryan rubs his eyes and writes out his routine report. He underlines it in red, reads it into the machine, sits down again before the log book.

He writes:

Another day has passed.

I am frightened, sometimes, that I am becoming too much of a vegetable. I am an active man by nature. I will need to be active when we land. I wonder if I have become too passive. Still, this is idle speculation . . .

His speculations were never idle, he reflects. The moment the problem was clearly seen, he began to think along positive lines. The problem was straightforward: society was breaking down and death and destruction were becoming increasingly widespread. He wished to survive and he wished for his friends and family to survive. There was nowhere in the world that could any longer be considered a safe refuge. Nuclear war was bound to arise soon. There had been only one answer: the stars. And there had been only one project for reaching the stars. Unmanned research craft had brought back evidence that there was a planetary system circling Barnard's Star and that two of those planets were in many respects similar to Earth.

The research project had been United Nations sponsored — the first important multilateral project between the Great Powers . . .

It had been a last attempt to draw the nations of the world together, to make them consider themselves one race.

Ryan shakes his head.

It had been too late, of course.

Ryan writes:

. . . I keep fit as best I can. An odd thought just popped into my head. It gives some idea of how closely one has to watch oneself. It occurred to me that a way of keeping fit would be to wake one of the other men so that we could have sparring matches, play football or something like that. I began to see the 'sense' of this and began to rationalise it so that it seemed advantageous to all concerned to wake, say, my brother John. Or even one of the women . . . There are several ways of keeping fit and alert — getting exercise. Ridiculous, undisciplined ideas! It is just as well I keep the log. It helps me keep perspective.

He grins. A great way of cheating on old John. He'd never know . . .

He shudders.

Naturally, he couldn't . . .

There was Josephine, too. It would betray the whole ideal of the mission if he betrayed them . . .

I think I'll go and take a cold shower! He writes jokingly. He signs the book, underlines his entry in red, closes the book, puts it neatly away, gets up, makes a last check of the instruments, asks the computer a couple of routine questions, is satisfied by the answers, leaves the control cabin.

True to his word, Mr Ryan has his cold shower. It does the trick. He feels much better. Humming to himself he enters his own cabin, selects the tape of Messiaen's Turangalila Symphony and sits down to listen to the strange and beautiful melodies of the Ondes Martenot.

By the Sixth Movement (*Jardin du sommeil d'amour*) he is asleep . . .

*

The gallery is vast and made of solid platinum.

He paces it.

It is the bridge of a massive ship. But the ship does not sail across the ocean. It sails through foliage. Dark, tangled foliage. Foliage that the Douanier himself might have painted. Menacing foliage.

Perhaps it is a jungle river. A river like the Amazon or one of those mysterious, unmapped rivers of New Guinea that, as a boy, he had wished to explore.

Ship . . . foliage . . . river . . .

He is alone on the ship, but for the sound of the engines, strangely melodic, and the cries of the unseen birds in the jungle.

He leans over the rail of the bridge, looking for the waters of the river. But there are no waters. Beneath the ship is only vegetation, crushed and bent by the passage of the great vessel.

The ship rolls.

He falls and from somewhere comes a sound that is oddly sympathetic. Something is pitying him.

He rejects the pity.

He falls to the ground and the ship passes on.

He is alone in the jungle and he hears the sounds of lumbering monsters in the murk. He searches with his eyes for the monsters, but he cannot see them, cannot trace the origin of their noise.

A woman appears. She is dark, lush, exotic. She parts her red lips and takes him by the hand into the shadowy darkness of the tropical foliage. Birds continue to cry and to squawk. He begins to kiss her wet, hot mouth. He feels her hand on his penis. He runs his hand into her crutch and her pants are wet with her juices. He

58

tries to make love to her, but for some reason she is wary, expecting discovery. She will not remove her clothing. They make love as best they can. Then she gets up and leads him through the dark jungle corridors into a clearing.

They are in a bar. Girls — club hostesses or prostitutes, he cannot tell — fill the place. There are a few men. Probably ponces or gigolos. He feels at ease here. He relaxes. He puts his arm around the dark woman and puts his other arm around a young blonde with a lined, decaying face. Someone he knew.

All the faces, in fact, are familiar. He tries to remember them. He concentrates on remembering them. Dimly he begins to remember them . . .

*

AFTER THE FAIR THEY WERE ALL LEAD
  Q: PLEASE DEFINE SPECIFIC SITUATION
ARDOUR THE MORE THEY SANG AHEAD
  Q: PLEASE DEFINE SPECIFIC SITUATION
AH DO RE ME FA SO LA TI DI
  Q: PLEASE DEFINE SPECIFIC SITUATION
ARIA ARIADNE ANIARA LEONARA CARMEN AMEN
  A: AMEN

*

AMEN.
  AMEN. AMEN. AMEN.
AMEN.

*

  SUGGEST HOLD ON TIGHT
  SUGGEST HOLD ON TIGHT
  SUGGEST HOLD ON TIGHT

*

```
KEEP GOING
E        O
E        O
P        I
         N
         N
G        G
O
I        K
N        E
         E
GOING KEEP
```

*

59

THE   SPACESHIP HOPE DEMPSEY IS EN ROUTE
       FOR MUNICH 15040 THE SPACESHIP
HOPE DEMPSEY IS EN ROUTE FOR MUNICH
         15040 IS GOING
EN ROUTE FOR MUNICH 15040 THE SPACE-
        SHIP NOWHERE
FOR   MUNICH   15040   THE   SPACESHIP
        MUST
HOPE DEMPSEY IS EN ROUTE BE
      SAFE
FOR   MUNICH   15040   MUST
THE   SPACESHIP
  KEEP   THEM
SPACESHIP
SAFE
  SPACESHIP
SPACE   SAFE
SHIP   KEEP THEM
SAFE   SAFE
SHIP   THE SPACESHIP HOPE DEMPSEY IS EN
SAFE   ROUTE FOR MUNICH 15040 AND
SHAPE   TRAVELLING AT POINT NINE OF C
SHIP   WE ARE ALL COMFORTABLE
SHAPE   WE ARE ALL
SPACE   SAFE
SHAPE   SPACESHIP SAFE
SHIP   SAFESHIPSAFE
SHAPE   SAFESHIPSHAPE

SAFE
SAFE
SAFE
SAFE
SAFE
SHIP
SHIP
SHIP
SHIP
SHAPE
SAFE
SHIP
SHIP
SAFE
SAFE
SHIP
SHIP
SAFE
SAFE
SHIP
SHIP
SAFE
SAFE
SHIP
SHIP
SAFE
SAFE
SHIP

SWEET
SAFE
SHIP
SPACE
SAIL
SPACE
SNAIL
PACE
SAFE
PACE
SNAIL
PACE
SPACE
SHIP
SAFE
PLACE
SPACE
SAFE
SMELL
TASTE
HASTE
RACE
WASTE
SPACE
SAVE
SPACE
SAFE
PLACE
SAFE CASE SPACE PLACE HATE HEAT SWEET SAFE

BRAIN
SHIP
TAME
WHIP
GOOD
TRIP
SPACE
SHIP
LET
RIP
SPACE
TRIP
HATE
TASTE
SPACE
FACE
HATE
HASTE
SPACE
RACE
HATE
FACE
SPACE
PLACE
HOT
DRIP
SPACE
SHIP
SHIP
HATE
HEAT SPACE HEAT SAFE FEAT SWEET HATE SAFE HAZE

NOT TRUE * * * * * * * *
NOT TRUE * * * * * * * *
* * * * * * * NOT TRUE *

*

NOT TRUE

*

'IT'S NOT FUCKING true!'
Ryan screams.
He wakes up.
The tape machine is humming rhythmically.
He shudders.
He has an erection.
His mouth is dry.
He has a pain above his left temple.
His legs are trembling.
His hands are gripping the plastic of his chair, pinching it in handfuls like a housewife inspecting a chicken.
The muscles at the back of his neck ache horribly.
He shakes his head.

*

What wasn't true?
The symphony has come to an end.
He gets up and switches off the machine, frowning and massaging his neck. He yawns.
Then he remembers the dream. The jungle. The women.
He grins with relief, recognising the source of the exclamation — the denial with which he had woken himself up.
Just simple, old-fashioned guilt feelings, obviously.
He had considered waking Janet, cheating on his brother, had dreamed accordingly, had denied his feelings and had come awake with a start.
All that proved was that he had a conscience.
He stretches.
Scratching his head he leaves the cabin and goes to take another shower.
As he washes, he smiles again. It's just as well to let those secret thoughts out into the open. No good burying them where they can fester into something much worse, catch him off his guard and possibly wreck the entire mission, maybe make him wake up the others. That would be fatal.

A wave of depression hits him. It's bloody hard, he thinks. Bloody.

He pulls himself together. His old reflexes are as good as ever. Keeping fit isn't just a matter of exercising the body. One has to exercise the brain, too. Make constant checks to be sure it's working smoothly.

He must be getting unduly sensitive, however, for his conscience was never that much of a burden to him!

He laughs. He knows what he must do.

It's the old trouble. The problem of leisure. It was unhealthy not to put your mind to something other than its own workings. He was developing the neuroses of the rich, the non-workers — or would start to, if he wasn't careful.

The dream is a warning.

Or rather his reaction to the dream is a warning. Tomorrow he will start studying the agricultural programmes, get interested in something other than himself.

Refreshed, his aches and pains vanishing, he returns to his cabin sorts out the agricultural programmes ready for the next day.

Then he goes to bed.

CHAPTER TWELVE

Although he is alone on board, he faithfully follows all the rituals as if there were a full crew in attendance.

As a boy I used to swim through cold water in the streams that ran between the pines, he thinks.

At the time set for the daily conferences, he sits at the head of the table and reviews the few events and projected tasks with which he is involved.

He eats at the formal meal times, uses formal language in all his dealings with the ship, makes formal checks and radios formal log entries back to Earth. His only break with formal routine is the red log-book he keeps in the desk.

He makes the formal tours to the Hibernation Section (nicknamed 'crew storage' by the personnel when they first came aboard).

As a young man I stood on hills in the wind and stared at moody skies, he thinks and I wrote awful, sentimental, self-pitying verse until the other lads found it and took the piss out of me so much I gave it up. I went into business instead. Just as well.

65

He touches the button and the spin screws automatically retract.

I wonder what would have happened to me. Art thrives in chaos. What's good for art isn't good for business ...

He pauses by the first container and looks into the patient face of his wife.

✱

Mrs Ryan cleaned down the walls of her apartment. She was using the appropriate fluid. All the time she cleaned she kept her face averted from the long window forming the far wall of the apartment.

When she had finished cleaning she took the can of fluid back to the kitchen and put it on the right shelf.

Frowning uncertainly, she stood in the middle of the kitchen.

Then she drew a deep breath and she reached towards the shelf again, touching another can. The can was labelled Plantfood.

She grasped the can.

She lifted it from the shelf.

She coughed and covered her mouth with her free hand.

She drew another breath.

She walked into the lobby and sprayed the orange tree that stood in its shining metallic tub. She went back to the living room, with its coloured walls, expensive, cushiony plastic chairs, the wall to wall TV.

She turned on the TV.

The wall opposite the window was instantly alive with whirling, dancing figures.

Watching them gyrate, Mrs Ryan relaxed a trifle. She looked at the can in her hand and put it down on the table. She watched the dancers. Her eyes were drawn back to the can, still lying on the table. She began to sit down. Then she stood up again.

Mrs Ryan's fresh forty-year-old face crumpled slightly. Her lips moved. She had the expression of a resolute but frightened child, half-ready to cry if the expected accident occurred.

She picked up the can and walked to the wall-long window. With her eyes half-closed she located the button which controlled the raising and lowering of the blinds. With the room in darkness she sprayed the plants on the windowsill.

She took the can back to the kitchen and placed it on the shelf. She stood in the kitchen doorway for a while, staring into the darkness of the living room, lit only by the flicker of the TV. Then she crossed the room to the window and placed her hand on the button controlling the blind.

She turned her back to the window and found the button with her left hand.

There was a big production number on TV. She stared at it, unmoving.

Then she pressed the button and sprang away from the window as the blinds rushed up and the room was flooded with daylight again.

She hurried into the kitchen, turning off the TV as she went past. She made some coffee and sat down to drink it.

The room was silent.

The empty window looked out on to the apartment block opposite. Their empty windows stared back.

Few cars ran in the street between the blocks.

Inside the apartment, in the kitchen, Mrs Ryan sat with her coffee cup raised like a puppet whose motor had cut out in mid-action.

The telephone buzzed.

Mrs Ryan sat still.

The telephone went on buzzing.

Mrs Ryan sighed and approached the instrument, set at head height on the kitchen wall. She ducked down against the wall and reached up to remove the mouthpiece.

'It's me. Uncle Sidney,' said the voice from the screen above her head.

'Oh, it's you, Uncle Sidney,' said Mrs Ryan. She backed away from the wall, still holding the mouthpiece and sat down near the kitchen table.

'Don't come too close,' said Uncle Sidney.

'Uncle Sidney,' said Mrs Ryan pitifully. 'I've asked you not to call during the day, when no one's at home. After all, I don't know who you are. It might be anyone.'

'I'm sorry I'm sure. I just wanted to ask if you'd like to come over tonight.'

'The car's being repaired,' said Mrs Ryan. 'He had to go by bus this morning. I told him not to, but he insisted. I don't know . . .'

Mrs Ryan broke off, a sadly bewildered look on her face.

There was silence.

Then she and Uncle Sidney spoke together:

'I've got to clean— ' Mrs Ryan said.

'Can't you come — ' said Uncle Sidney.

'Uncle Sidney. I've got to clean the front door today. And I know — I *know* that as soon as I open the door the woman from the next apartment will come out and pretend she's going to use the garbage disposal. Do you realise what it's like living next to a woman like that?'

Uncle Sidney's lined face dropped. 'Well, if you won't visit your uncle you won't,' he said. 'Do you know how long it's been since I saw you and him and the kids? Three months.'

'I'm sorry, Uncle Sidney.' Mrs Ryan looked at the floor, noticing a smear on one of the tiles. 'You wouldn't come to see us, I suppose . . . ?'

'On my own?' Uncle Sidney said contemptuously.

He cut the connection. Mrs Ryan sat by the kitchen table holding the mouthpiece in her hand. She stood up slowly and replaced it.

It seemed to her that she could not get the cleaner and the spray from the cupboard. She could not cross the kitchen and go through the living room into the lobby. She could not, alone, open the front door.

She could not open the front door.

She might . . .

Mrs Ryan's mind became dark, fearful, confused.

She was swept around the whirlpool of her brain, helpless and still, in spite of herself, struggling.

She could not open the door.

She could not.

Mrs Ryan uttered a low moan and went into the bedroom.

Even in daylight the walls shimmered with many colours. The bed was neatly covered with the white bedspread. The shining dressing table was clear. Mrs Ryan picked up the only sign of occupancy, a pair of Mr Ryan's outdoor shoes. She opened a concealed cupboard and threw them in violently. She ran to the window, pressed the button on the sill.

The blinds came down quickly.

The walls of the room glowed and flickered.

Mrs Ryan paced to and fro. Past the bed to the darkened window. Back from the window to the bed. Back and forth.

She stopped and turned on soft, soothing music.

She ran out of the room and locked the front door.

She came back into the bedroom, shut that door, lay down on the bed, listening to the music.

Even the music seemed slightly harsh today.

She closed her eyes and the faces came. She opened her eyes and

68

reached towards the bedside cupboard, took out her sleeping pills, swallowed a pill and lay down again.

The music was almost raucous. She turned it off.

She lay in silence, waiting for sleep.

It was 11.23 a.m.

CHAPTER THIRTEEN

Mrs Ryan began to dream.

She was walking across the field away from the house she had lived in when she was eight. If she turned round she could see her mother framed in the kitchen window, her head bent over the stove. Behind her she could hear shouts of her brothers playing hide-and-seek.

Mrs Ryan trod over the springy turf, dreamily floated over the bright grass. She could hear birds singing in the trees at the edges of the field.

Mrs Ryan was floating, floating over the fields, far from the house. How sunny it was. How the birds sang. She was walking again. She turned to look for the house but she was too far away. She could not see it. The sky was darkening. She could only dimly see the trees on either side of the field. She seemed to hear a noise; a babble of talk. At once, ahead of her, she saw a dark crowd approaching, talking among themselves. As they came closer she could still not distinguish one person from another. She had the impression that there were men, women and children. But the mass was still a dark blurr of heads, bodies, limbs, formless and faceless. The crowd advanced, the cackle of voices growing louder.

She stood transfixed in the field.

She could not move.

And the voices grew clearer.

'Look. There she is. She's there. She's really there.'

She felt the mood of the crowd change.

She felt a terrible fear.

'She's there. That's her. That's her. She's there. She's there.

She stood rooted to the spot, her legs too heavy to carry her.

'She's there. She's there. That's her. That's her.'

The dark crowd began to run towards her. It yelled and cried out. She could hear high, vengeful screams from the women. The crowd was almost on her.

And Mrs Ryan woke with a start in her bedroom in the light of the shimmering walls. She looked at the clock.

It was 11.31 a.m.

Trembling she lay there on the white bedspread, fighting her way out of the dream. She gazed blankly at the walls, blinking her eyes to rid herself of the image of the black, blank faces of that terrible crowd. She rose and walked heavily from the room.

She went into the kitchen and took a pill to clear her head. Sighing, she removed the can of cleaner from the shelf, walked through the living room, out into the lobby and up to the front door. She put her hand on the latch.

Mrs Ryan hesitated, stiffened her back and opened the front door. She crept outside, into the long corridor.

The corridor was bright and white. It stretched away from her on either side. Set in the walls were the doors, all painted in fresh, dark colours.

Slowly Mrs Ryan began to spray the cleaner on the surface of the door. Once the door was covered with the white film she began to rub it off, faster and faster.

Nearly done, she thought to herself, nearly done. Thank God, thank God. Soon finished. Thank God.

Very slowly the blue door of the apartment opposite began to open. A woman looked through the crack of the door. She and Mrs Ryan stared at each other in shock. The woman's hand went to her mouth. Mrs Ryan recovered herself first.

Leaving the door half covered in white cleaning fluid she ran back inside her apartment and slammed the door. Almost at the same moment the other woman shut her own door.

Mrs Ryan stood in the middle of her kitchen, gasping for breath. 'That bitch,' she said aloud. 'That bitch. What does she want to persecute me for? Why does she always do that to me? Spying on me all the time. Bitch, bitch, bitch.'

She went to the shelf, took down a bottle of capsules and swallowed two. She went into the living room and fell down on the plastic couch. She switched on the TV.

There was a picture of a family eating a turkey dinner. The turkey and its trimmings were laid out brightly on a gay table. The family — parents and three teenage children — were joking. Mrs Ryan watched the programme with a faint smile curling round her mouth.

She was soon alseep.

It was 11.48 a.m.

70

The boys woke her up.

She told them what had happened and they told Ryan.

Ryan was sympathetic.

'You need a holiday, old girl,' he said. 'We'll see what we can do.'

'I'd rather not,' she said. 'I prefer to stay at home. It's just — the *interference* from the neighbours. I'm proud of my home.'

'Of course you are. We'll see what we can do.'

It was 7.46 p.m.

'Time passes so slowly,' she said.

'It depends how you look at it,' he replied.

*

She suffered a lot, thinks Ryan. *Maybe I could have been more helpful.*

He shrugs the thought off. A pointless exercise. There was nothing to be gained from self-recrimination. If one didn't like what one had done, the best thing was to decide not to do it again and leave it at that. That was the pragmatic attitude. The scientific attitude.

He looks down at the sleeping face of his wife and he smiles tenderly, touching the top of the container.

Even her condition improved once they had decided on their goal. She was basically a sensible woman. Her condition was no different from that of millions of others in the cities all over the world.

If they had taken one of the abandoned houses in the country, perhaps she would have been happier. But probably not. The isolation of the places beyond the cities was pretty unbearable.

She had liked the country as a girl, of course. That was partly what the dream was about, he guessed. That dream of hers. It had recurred relatively frequently. Not unlike that recurring dream of his.

He starts to pace between the containers, checking them automatically.

What is Time, after all? Do we meet in our dreams?

Pointless, mystical speculation.

*

Everything seems to be in order. The containers are functioning correctly. Ryan yawns and stretches, fighting off the sinking feeling in his stomach, ignoring the impulse to wake at least some of the occupants of the containers. They must not be awakened until the ship nears the planet that is its destination.

71

This is his penance, his test, his reward.

*

He has one last look at his sleeping boys, then he leaves the compartment and makes his way back to the main control cabin, sends his report back to Earth. All is well aboard the spaceship *Hope Dempsey*.

He writes a short entry in his red log-book:

On the other side of those thin walls is infinite space. There is no life for billions of miles. No man has ever been more alone.

*

In his cabin he takes three pills, disposes of his clothes, lies down.

As he begins to fall asleep a numb, desperate feeling tells him that tonight could be another of those nights of fitful, nightmare-ridden sleep. His routine demands that he sleep regularly. His health will break if he does not. Ryan lies on his narrow couch willing himself not to rise. The pills take effect and Ryan sleeps.

*

He dreams that he is in his office. It is dark. He has drawn the blinds to shut out the city noise and the view of the shining office towers opposite. He sits at his desk doing nothing. His hands are curled on the desk before him. The fingernails are torn. He is afraid.

He sees his wife in their flat. She is sitting in the darkened living-room doing nothing.

He sees the bedroom in which his two sons lie sleeping under heavy sedation. The youngest, five-year-old Alexander, groans in his sleep, thrusts an arm, thin as a Foreigner's, out of the covers. The arm dangles lifelessly down from his bed. He moans again. His brother Rupert, who is twelve, lies on his back, eyes half open in his coma, staring blindly at the ceiling.

Back in the living-room Ryan sees the hunched figure of his wife. Again he sees himself sitting at his office desk staring into the half dark.

The family is waiting.

It is waiting in fear.

It does not know what to expect.

It knows that it will come from the others.

There is a scratching noise behind him. Ryan, half-paralysed with terror, turns slowly round to see what it is. He faces the window now. The blind is shaking, as if it were being blown by the wind. There is something behind the blind, something from outside, trying to enter the office. Ryan breathes in, holds his breath hard in some animal instinct to make himself so immobile that he will not be noticed. The blind shakes and shakes. A bony hand comes through the fabric, leaving no gap or tear, merely sliding through as if the material were smoke, or air. Ryan gazes at the hand. It belongs to an old woman, thin fingered, with pronounced tendons. The nails are painted red. There are three large rings; two diamond ones on the middle finger, a large amethyst on the slender, slightly curved, little finger. The hand appears to part the blind and a face peers in.

It is the face of an old woman. The wrinkled eyelids are carefully painted blue. The mouth is blackened, the lined cheeks powdered. The old woman looks Ryan straight in the eyes and smiles, revealing yellow teeth, the edges slightly serrated with age. Ryan stares at the old woman. She continues to give him a confidential, intimate smile.

Her hand appears again, through another part of the blind.

It holds a pair of round, dark glasses.

The hand moved towards her face. It places the glasses over her eyes. Then the hand disappears through the blind again, leaving no gap or rent in it.

The old, blackened mouth continues to smile below the obliterated eyes.

Then the old woman's face, in the centre of the blind, begins to droop. The smile disappears, the lips begin to curve in a snarl.

Ryan is terrified.

He cannot scream.

He wants to say the following words:

I — DID — NOT

— but he cannot.

He cannot say the . . .

I ——

He gets up from his bed. He is sweating. Naked, he leaves the cabin and walks down the bright corridor, enters the main control cabin and stares at the dancing, shifting indicators, at the ever busy computer.

He listens to the faint hum of the engine which is propelling the little pellet of steel through the void.

The computer has left him a message. He walks over to the machine and reads it.

It says:

*******THERE IS A LOSS OF COMMUNICATION*******

73

*********9876543210000000000000`````````````````````````/***********
****A LOSS**"""""""""""""PLEASE ENSURE THAT IN
FUTURE***INFORMATION IS GIVEN IN THE CORRECT
FORM"""""""REPEAT   THE**CORRECT   FORM"""""""""""
WHAT IS THE EXACT NATURE OF THE******SITUA-
TION REPEAT WHAT IS THE EXACT NATURE OF THE**
SITUATION REPEAT WHAT IS THE EXACT NATURE OF
THE*******SITUATION """""""""""""""""""""**************

Uncomprehendingly Ryan stares at the message.

What has gone wrong?

He has carried out his duties impeccably.

His days have been dedicated to order, the routine of the ship.

What has he done wrong?

Or — worse — what mistake can be occurring inside the computer?

He rips off the printout and reads it, seeking a clue. It has all the fluency and random lack of sense of a message from a ouija board.

And as he reads the computer spills out more:

******I CANNOT READ YOUR LAST MESSAGE UNLESS
**********INFORMATION IS GIVEN IN THE CORRECT
FORM"""""I CANNOT**ASSIST"""""""PLEASE REPEAT
YOUR LAST MESSAGE IN THE****CORRECT FORM****

Wearily Ryan organises the machine to rerun his last message. It reads:

*******TRIUMPHANT IN THE BLOODY SKY AND
THE HUMAN FORM*IS NO MORE******************

I must control this sort of thing, thinks Ryan.

He wanders to the desk and takes out his red log-book. He writes:

I must keep better control of things.

He struggles back to the computer and realises he has left his red log-book on the desk. He weaves back to the desk and carefully, but with great difficulty, puts the book in its drawer. Slowly, he closes the door. He returns to the computer. He erases the messages as best he can by condemning them to the computer's deepest memory cells. He walks wearily from the control room.

I must control this sort of thing.

I must forget these nightmares.

I must maintain order.

It could wreck the computer and then I would be finished.

Everything depends on me.

Triumphant in the bloody sky and the human form . . .

74

Ryan weeps.

He paces the corridor, back to his prison, takes three more pills and sleeps.

He dreams of the factory. A huge hall, somewhat darker in Ryan's dream than it was in reality. It is filled with large silent machines. Only the throbbing of the tiled floor indicates the activity of the machines.

At the end of each machine is a large drum into which spill the parts used in the making of Ryan Toys.

There are the smooth heads, legs, arms and torsos of dolls; the woolly heads, legs and torsos of lambs, tigers and rabbits; the metal legs, heads and torsos of mechanical puppets. There are the tiny powerpacs for the bellies of Ryan Toys; there are the metal parts for Ryan Toys dredgers, oilpumps, spacecraft; there are the great, shining grinning heads of Rytoy Realboys and Rytoy Realgirls; the great probosces of Rytoy Realphants.

The vast machines turn out their parts steadily and inexorably. As each drum fills it glides away and is replaced by another which is, in turn, steadily filled.

Ryan is a witness to this scene. He knows that he will be involved if they find out.

He sees a white-coated mechanic walk along the files of machines and disappear through a door at the end of the hall.

Did the mechanic notice him?

The drums roll away and are replaced by empty ones.

Suddenly Ryan sees the parts rise, as if in weightlessness. They join together, assembling in mid-air. As each toy is completed, or as completed as it can be with the parts available, it sinks to the floor of the hall and begins to operate.

A row of golden haired Realboys, lifesize but armless, revolve slowly, singing *Frère Jacques* in their high voices.

A cluster of woolly lambs gambol mechanically, raising and dipping their heads.

On the floor the large trunks of the Realphants plunge and rise.

The spacecraft hover a foot above the floor, emitting humming noises.

Ryrobots strut and clank about, running into the machines and toppling over. Two great heaps of musical building blocks chime out the letters printed on their sides —

I AM *A*

I AM *M*

I AM *U*

The piles fall and tumble as Ryan kicks them.

The Realgirls link hands and dance around him, tossing their blonde curls. The Ryan Battlewagons run about the floor, shooting their miniature missiles.

Ryan looks fondly at the action, music and chatter of his toys. The whole of the tiled floor is being gradually covered with toys in motion. All these things are Ryan's — made and sold by Ryan.

He looks at the building blocks and smiles. Some have fallen and spelled out: AMUSEMENT.

In the middle of this cheerful scene, Ryan ceases to dream and falls fast asleep.

*

In accordance with the regulations ensuring that no member of the government or the civil service could be identified save by his rank (thus ensuring the absence of blackmail, bribery, favour seeking and/or giving and so forth) the Man from the Ministry wore a black cloth over his face. It had neat holes for his eyes and his mouth.

Ryan, sitting behind his office desk, contemplated the Man from the Ministry somewhat nervously.

'Will you have a cup of tea?' he asked.

'I think not.'

Ryan could almost see the expression of suspicious distaste on the man's face. He had made a tactical blunder.

'Ah . . .' said Ryan.

'Mr Ryan . . .' began the official.

'Yes,' said Ryan, as if in confirmation. 'Yes, indeed.'

'Mr Ryan — you seem unaware that this country is in a state of war . . .'

'Ah. No.'

'Since Birmingham launched its completely unprovoked attack on London, Mr Ryan, and bombed the reservoirs of Shepperton and Staines, the official government of South England has had to requisition a great deal of private industry if it has been discovered that it has not been contributing to our war effort as efficiently as it might . . .'

'That's a threat, is it?' Ryan said thickly.

'A friendly tip, Mr Ryan.'

'We've turned over as fast as we can,' Ryan explained. 'We *were* a bloody toy factory, you know. Overnight we had to change to manufacturing weapon parts and communications equipment. Naturally we haven't had a completely smooth ride. On the other hand, we've done our best . . .'

'Your production is not up to scratch, Mr Ryan. I wonder if your heart is in the war effort? Some people do not seem to realise that the old society has been swept away, that the Patriots are bent on ordering an entirely new kind of nation now that the remnants of the alien groups have been pushed back beyond the Thames. Though attacked from all sides, though sustaining three hydrogen bomb drops from France, the Patriots have managed to hold this land of ours together. They can only do it with the full co-operation of people like yourself, Mr Ryan.'

'We aren't getting the raw materials,' Ryan said. 'Half the things we need don't arrive. It's a bloody shambles!'

'That sounds like a criticism of the government, Mr Ryan.'

'You know I'm a registered Patriot supporter.'

'Not all registered supporters have remained loyal, Mr Ryan.'

'Well, I *am* loyal!' Ryan half believed himself as he shouted at the Man from the Ministry. He and the group had decided early on that the Patriots would soon hold the power and had taken the precaution of joining the party. 'It's just that we can't work more than ten bloody miracles a day!'

'You've got a week, I'm afraid, Mr Ryan.' The official got up, closing his briefcase. 'And then it will be a Temporary Requisition Order until our borders are secure again.'

'You'll take over?'

'You will continue to manage the factory, if you prove efficient. You will enjoy the status of any other civil servant.'

Ryan nodded. 'What about compensation?'

'Mr Ryan,' said the official grimly, wearily, 'there is a dis-credited cabinet that fled to Birmingham to escape retribution. Among other things that was discovered about that particular cabinet was that it was corrupt. Industrialists were lining their pockets with the connivance of government officials. That sort of thing is all over now. All over. Naturally, you will receive a receipt guaranteeing the return of your business when the situation has been normalised. We hope, however, that it won't have to happen. Keep trying, Mr Ryan. Keep trying. Good luck to you.'

Ryan watched the official leave. He would have to warn the group that things were moving a little faster than anticipated.

He wondered how things were in the rest of the world. Very few reports came through these days. The United States were now Dis-united and at war. United Europe had fragmented into thousands of tiny principalities, rather as England had. As for Russia and the Far East the only information he had had for months was that a horde thousands of times greater than the Golden Horde was sweeping in all directions. Possibly none of the information was true. He hoped that the town of Surgut on the Siberian Plain was still untouched. Everything depended on that.

Ryan got up and left the office.

It was time to go home.

CHAPTER FOURTEEN

When he awakes he feels relieved, alert and refreshed. He eats his breakfast as soon as he has exercised and walks to the control room where he runs through all the routine checks and adjustments until lunch-time.

After lunch he goes to the little gym behind the main control cabin and vaults and climbs and swings until it is time to inspect Hibernation.

He unlocks the door of Hibernation and makes a routine and unemotional check. A minor alteration is required in the rate of fluid flow on Number Seven container. He makes the alteration.

Again the routine checks, the reiteration during the normal conference period.

He then does two hours study of the agricultural programmes. He learns a great deal. It is a much more interesting subject that he would have guessed.

Then it is time to report to the computer and read the log through to Earth, if anyone is left on Earth to hear it.

He makes the last of his reports for this period:

'Day number one thousand four hundred and sixty-six. Spaceship Hope Dempsey en route for Munich 15040. Speed steady at point nine of *c*. All systems functioning according to original expectations. No other variations. All occupants are comfortable and in good health.'

Ryan goes to the desk and takes out his red log-book. He frowns. Scrawled across a page are the words:

I MUST KEEP BETTER CONTROL OF THINGS

It hardly looks like his writing. Yet it must be.

And when did he write it? He has not had time to make any entries in the log until now. It could have been at any time today. Or last night. He frowns. When . . . ?

He cannot remember.

He takes a deep breath and he rules two heavy red lines under the entry, writes the date below it and begins:

All continues well. I maintain my routine and am hopeful for the future. Today I feel less bedevilled by loneliness and have more confidence in my ability to carry out my mission. Our ship carries us steadily onwards. I am confident that all is well. I am confident ——

He stops writing and scratches his head, staring at the phrase above the entry.

I MUST KEEP CONTROL OF THINGS

I am confident that my period of nightmares and near-hysteria is over. I have regained control of myself and therefore ——

He considers tearing out this page and beginning it afresh. But that would not be in accord with the regulations he is following. He sucks his lower lip . . .

am doubtless much more cheerful. The above phrase is something of a puzzle to me, for at this point I cannot remember writing it. Perhaps I was under even greater stress than I imagined and wrote it last night after finishing the ordinary entry. Well, it was good advice — the advice of this stranger who could only have been myself!

It gives me a slightly eery feeling, however, I must admit. I expect I will remember when I wrote it. I hope so. In the meantime there is no point in my racking my brains. The information will come when my unconscious is ready to let me have it!

Otherwise — all O.K. The gloom and doom period is over — at least for the time being. I am in a thoroughly constructive and balanced state of mind.

He signs off with a flourish and, humming, puts the book in the desk, closes the drawer, gets up, takes a last look around the control room and goes out into the passage.

Before returning to his cabin, he goes to the library and gets a couple of educational tapes.

In his cabin, he studies the programmes for a while and then goes to sleep.

He dreams again.

He is on the new planet. A pleasant landscape. A valley. With some sort of digging instrument he is working the soil. He is alone and at peace. There is no sign of the spaceship or of the other occupants. This does not worry him. He is alone and at peace.

*

Next morning he continues with his routine work. He eats, he makes his formal log entries, he manages to get an extra hour of study. He is beginning to understand the principles of agriculture.

He returns to the control room to make the last of his reports — the standard one — which, according to his routine, he first enters in his log-book and then reads out to the computer. He then sits down and picks up his stylus to begin his private entry. He enters the date.

Another pleasant and uneventful day spent largely in the pursuit of knowledge! I am beginning to feel like some old scholar. I can understand the attraction, suddenly, in the pursuit of information for its own sake. In a way, of course, it is an escape — I can see that even the most sophisticated sort of academic activity is at least in part a rejection of the realities of ordinary living. My studies, naturally, are perfectly practical, in that I will need a great deal of knowledge about every possible kind of agriculture when we

The computer is flashing a signal. It wants his attention.

Frowning, Ryan gets up and goes over to the main console.

He reads the computer's message.

*******CONDITION OF OCCUPANTS OF CONTAINERS NOT*****REPORTED********************************

Ryan gasps. It is true. For the first time he has not checked the Hibernation compartment. He realises now that he was so caught up in his studies he must have forgotten. He replies to the computer:

******REPORT FOLLOWS SHORTLY******************

Reproving himself for this stupid lapse, relieved that the computer is programmed to check every function he performs and to remind him of any oversights, he marches along the corridor to the Hibernation room.

He touches the stud to open the door.

But the door remains closed.

He presses the stud harder.

Still the door does not open.

Ryan feels a moment's panic. Could there be someone else aboard the ship? A stowaway of some kind who . . . ?

He rejects the notion as stupid. And then he returns to the main control cabin and gives the computer a question.

******HIBERNATION COMPARTMENT DOOR WILL NOT OPEN*****PLEASE ADVISE**********************

There is a pause before the computer replies:

******EMERGENCY LOCK EFFECTIVE"""""""""YOU MUST*********DEACTIVATE AT MAIN CONSOLE*****

Ryan licks his lips and goes to the main console. He scans the door plan and sees that the computer is correct. He touches a stud on the console and cuts off the emergency lock. Was the mistake his or the computer's. Perhaps the emergency lock was activated at the same time as he made the mysterious log entry.

He returns to the Hibernation room and opens the door.

He enters the compartment.

CHAPTER FIFTEEN

The containers gleam a pure, soft white.

He walks to the first and inspects it. It contains his wife.

*

JOSEPHINE RYAN 9.9.1960. 7.3.2004.

*

His blonde, pink-faced wife, blue eyes peacefully closed, lies in her green fluid. She looks so natural that Ryan half expects her to open her eyes and smile at him. Josephine, heart of the ship, so glad to be setting out on her great adventure, so glad to be free from the torture of living in the city with its unbearable atmosphere of hostility.

Ryan smiles as he remembers the eager step with which she came aboard on the day of the take-off, how she had lost, almost overnight, the sadness and the fear which had afflicted her — indeed, which had been afflicting them all. He sighs. How pleasant to be together again.

*

RUPERT RYAN. 13.7.1990. 6.3.2004.

*

ALEXANDER RYAN. 25.12.1996. 6.3.2004.

*

Ryan walks fairly quickly past the containers where his two sons' immature faces gaze in startlement at the bright ceiling.

*

SYDNEY RYAN. 2.2.1937. 25.12.2003.

*

Ryan stares for a while at the wrinkled old face, lips slightly drawn back over the false teeth, the thin muscley old shoulders showing above the plastic sheet drawn over the main length of the containers.

*

JOHN RYAN. 15.8.1963. 26.12.2003.

*

ISABEL RYAN. 22.6.1962. 13.2.2004.

*

Isabel. Still weary looking, even though at peace . . .

*

JANET RYAN. 10.11.1982. 7.5.2004.

*

Ah, Janet, thinks Ryan with a surge of affection.
He loved Josephine. But, by God, he loved Janet passionately.
He frowned. The problem had not been over when they went into Hibernation. It would take a great deal of self-discipline on his part to make sure that it did not start all over again.

*

FRED MASTERSON. 4.5.1950. 25.12.2003.

*

TRACY MASTERSON. 29.10.1973. 9.10.2003.

*

JAMES HENRY. 4.3.1957. 29.10.2003.

*

IDA HENRY. 3.3.1980. 1.2.2004.

*

FELICITY HENRY. 3.3.1980. 1.2.2004.

*

Everything is as it should be. Everybody is sleeping peacefully. Only Ryan is awake.
He blinks.

Only Ryan is awake because it is better for one man to suffer acute loneliness and isolation than for several to live in tension.

One strong man.

Ryan raises his eyebrows.

And leaves Hibernation.

*

Ryan reports to the computer:

JOSEPHINE RYAN. CONDITION STEADY.

RUPERT RYAN CONDITION STEADY.

ALEXANDER RYAN. CONDITION STEADY.

SIDNEY RYAN. CONDITION STEADY.

JOHN RYAN. CONDITION STEADY.

ISABEL RYAN. CONDITION STEADY.

JANET RYAN.

      CONDITION STEADY.

       FRED MASTERSON. CONDITION STEADY.

     TRACY MASTERSON. CONDITION

              STEADY.

   JAMES

              HENRY

CONDITION STEADY.

IDA HENRY. CONDITION STEADY.

     FELICITY HENRY. CONDITION

   STEADY.

The computer says:

******EARLIER YOU REPORTED YOURSELF LONELY*
''''''''''''DOES THIS CONDITION STILL OBTAIN***

Ryan replies:

******CONDITION EASIER SINCE THEN**************

He moves to his desk and picks up his diary.

He writes:

land.

A short while ago the computer reported an oversight of mine. I'd forgotten to report on the condition of the personnel. The first time I've done anything like that! And the last, I hope. Then I discovered that the emergency locks in Hibernation had been sealed and I had to come back and unseal them. I must have done that, too, when I made the above entry. I feel relaxed and at ease now. The previous mistakes and, I suppose, mild blackouts must have been the result of the strain which I now seem to have overcome.

Ryan winds up the entry, closes the log, puts it away, leaves the control room.

He goes to his cabin and sets aside the educational tapes. *Too much concentration*, he thinks. *Mustn't overdo it. It's incredible how one has to watch the balance. A very delicate equilibrium involved here. Very delicate.*

He starts to watch an old Patriot propaganda play about the discovery of a cell of the Free Yorkshire underground and its eventual elimination.

He turns it off.

He hears something. He turns his head from the viewer.

It is a year since he heard a footstep not his own.

But now he can hear footsteps.

He sits there, feeling sweat prickle under his hair, listening to what seems to be the sound of echoing steps in the passage outside.

There is some stranger aboard!

He listens as the steps approach the door of the compartment. Then they pass.

He forces himself out of his chair and gets to the door. He touches the stud to open the door. It opens slowly.

Outside the passageway stretches on both sides, the length of the ship's crew quarters. The only sound is the faint hum of the ship's system.

Ryan gets a glass of water and drinks it.

He switches the viewer back on, half smiling. Typical auditory hallucination of a lonely man, he thinks. The programme ends.

Ryan decides to get some exercise.

He leaves his cabin and makes for the gym.

As he walks along the corridor he feels footsteps moving behind him. He ignores the feeling with a shrug.

Then comes a moment's panic. He gives way to the impulse to turn sharply.

There is, of course, no one there.

Ryan reaches the gym. He has the impression that he is being watched as he runs through his exercises.

He lies down on a couch for fifteen minutes before beginning the second half of the exercise routine.

He remembers family holidays on the Isle of Skye. That was in the very early years, of course, before Skye was taken over as an experimental area for research into algae food substitutes. He remembers the pleasant evenings he and Josephine used to have with Tracy and Fred Masterson. He remembers the evening walks through the roof gardens with his wife. He remembers Christmases, he remembers sunsets. He remembers the smell of the rain on the fields of the place where he was born. He remembers the smell of his toy factories — the hot metal, the paint, the freshly cut timber. He remembers his mother. She had been one of the victims of the short-lived Hospitals Euthenasia Act. The Act had been repealed by the Nimmoites during their short period of power. The only sensible thing they did, thinks Ryan.

He sleeps.

Once again he is on the planet, in the valley. But this time he is panic-stricken that the ship and the others have left him. He begins to run. He runs into the jungle. He sees a dark woman. He is in his own toy factory among the dancing toys.

He takes pleasure at the sight of these things he has made. They all function together so joyfully. He sees the musical building blocks. They still spell out a word.

AMU . . .

With dawning fear he hears, above the bangs and clangs of the mechanical toys, the drone of the dirge-like music which in other dreams accompanies the dancers in the darkened ballroom.

The music rises, almost drowning out the sounds made by the moving toys. Ryan feels himself standing rooted with fear in the middle of his gyrating models. The music grows louder. The toys spin to and fro, round and round. They begin to climb on top of each other, lamb on dredger, girl doll on piles of bricks, making a huge pyramid close to him. The pyramid grows and grows until it is at the level of his eyes. The music grows louder and louder.

In his terror Ryan anticipates a point in the music when the pyramid of still moving toys collapses on him.

He struggles to free himself from the toils of little mechanical bodies.

As he struggles he awakes. He lies there and hears himself groan:
'I thought they were over. I've got to do something about it.'

He gets off the couch and abandons the idea of exercise.

He stares around at the exercising machines. 'I can remain master of myself,' Ryan says.

'I can.'

He goes back to the control room, adjusts various dials, checks that his time devices are working accurately and makes the following statement to the computer:
*******I AM TROUBLED BY NIGHTMARES***********

The computer replies:
******I KNOW THIS''''''''''''INJECT 1 CC PRODITOL PER*
DIEM'''''''''''''DO NOT TAKE MORE'''''''''''''DISCONTINUE
THE DOSE**AS SOON AS POSSIBLE AND AT ALL COSTS

Ryan rubs his lips.

Then he bites the nail of his right forefinger.

*

Ryan paces the ship.

Passageways, engine room, supplies room, exercise room, control room, own cabin, spare cabins, observation room, library . . .

He does not look at the door of the Hibernation room. He does not walk along the passage towards the door.

He continues his angry prowling for half an hour or more, trying to collect his thoughts.

The footsteps follow him most of the time. Footsteps he knows do not exist.

Echoing up and down the passageways he begins to hear fragments of the voices of his companions, the men and women now suspended in green fluid in the containers that must remain sealed until planetfall.

'Daddy! Daddy!' cries his youngest child Alexander.

Ryan hears the thud of his feet in the passage. He overhears an argument between Ida and Felicity Henry: 'Don't keep telling me how you feel. I don't want to know,' Felicity snaps at her pregnant twin sister. 'You don't realise what it's like,' says the other on a familiar note of complaint. 'No, no. I don't,' he hears Felicity say hysterically. He hears the noise of a slap and Ida's weeping. A door bangs. 'Let me see to it, Ryan,' he hears James Henry say impatiently. The voice seems to echo all over the ship. He hears Fred and Tracy Masterson's feet coming rapidly along the passageway. His wife Josephine is behind them. 'Daddy! Daddy!' The child's feet come scudding up to him. Ryan turns his head this way and that. Where are the sounds coming from?

Janet Ryan sings, far away.

'Homeward bound, where the fields are like honey . . .'

Ryan cannot hear the words properly. He cranes his neck to listen, but the words are still indistinct. Uncle Sidney is singing too. 'There was a man who had a mouse, hi-diddle-um-tum-ti-do; he baked it in an apple pie; there was a man who had a mouse . . .'

Isabel Ryan's voice comes from somewhere around him. 'I can't bear any more!'

Then the rumble of John Ryan, his brother, talking to her, saying something Ryan cannot catch.

Janet singing.

Both boys are running, running, running . . .

And Ryan, in the centre of all this noise, sinks to the floor of the passage, cocks his head, listening to the voices.

As he crouches there it seems to him that the voices must be coming from the room at the end of the passage. Automatically he gets to his feet and with a stiff gait starts to walk up the passageway towards the door.

The voices grow louder.

'I hate to see a man playing at being indispensible. It benefits neither him nor the people about him,' says James Henry.

'The Lord thy God is a jealous God and thou shalt have no other God than Him,' advises Uncle Sidney.

'Never mind, dear, never mind,' Isobel Ryan is telling someone.

Alexander is crying muffled sobs into the pillow.

Janet Ryan is singing in her high, clear voice: 'Homeward bound, we're homeward bound, where the singing birds welcome such lovers as we . . .'

Ida and Felicity Henry are still arguing: 'Take it.' 'I don't want to take it.' 'You must take it. It's what you need.' 'I know what I need.' 'Be sensible. Drink it now.'

As Ryan reaches the door, the voices rise. As he touches the stud, they are louder still.

Conversations, statements, songs, sobs, laughter, arguments, all coming towards him in an indistinguishable medley.

Then the door is open.

The noises cease abruptly and Ryan is left in the silence, staring at the thirteen containers, twelve full and labelled with the names and dates of the occupants.

The owners of the voices lie there quietly in their pale fluid. Ryan stands there in the doorway, suddenly realising again that he is alone, that the noise has ceased, that he has opened the door at an unscheduled time . . .

His companions continue to sleep. Peaceful and unaware of the torment he is undergoing, they are all at CONDITION STEADY.

Which is more than I am, thinks Ryan. Tears come to his eyes.

From the door he cannot see the people in the containers.

He counts the containers. There are still thirteen. He looks at the thirteenth, his own. He draws in his breath. His lips curl back in a frightened, feral snarl. He steps out into the passageway and slams the heel of his hand against the door, shutting it.

He begins to run very slowly down the passage until he comes to the end.

Then he leans against a bulkhead, breathing heavily.

He gasps and gasps again. Then he straightens his back and sets off slowly for the control room.

I shall have to think about that injection. I might not be able to carry on without it. I'd hoped to hold out longer than this. Doesn't do to get too reliant on that sort of thing. It is supposed to be addictive, after all.

Maybe one dose will do the trick. One might be all I need.

At any rate, I daren't go on without it.

Ryan decides to have his first injection the next morning.

The Proditol is an enzyme-inhibiting substance that works directly on new cell matter entering the brain. It has the effect of preventing the release of harmful substances into the cells, causing lack of connection with the outside world and, thus, delusions. Ryan, partly for pride's sake, partly for reasons he does not fully understand, is very unwilling to take the drug.

But Ryan is dedicated to the ship, its occupants, its goal.

There is little he would not do in order to be able to continue with the steady schedule of the ship and fulfill his responsibility towards its occupants.

Ryan has made his decision.

Plenty of sleeping pills tonight and the Proditol tomorrow.

He goes to his sleeping compartment but then wanders back to the main control room.

He asks for details of the action of the drug.

*******ICC PRODITOL " " " ICC PRODITOL ALSO MA—19cccUSSR* ICC PRODITOL IS A FAST ACTING DRUG OF THE ENZYME******INHIBITOR VARIETY " " " " " " " IT BEGINS TO TAKE EFFECT***** WITHIN TEN MINUTES OF INJECTION " " " " " " " ITS FULL EFFECT* IS FELT WITHIN THE HOUR FOLLOWING " " " " " " AFTER THIS**** THE MIND OF THE PATIENT SHOULD BE RELIEVED OF ALL**** IMPRESSIONS OF A DELUSORY NATURE " " " " " " IN THE*********SEVEREST CASES THE DRUG WILL CONTROL ADVERSE*********SYMPTOMS FOR 24 HOURS AFTER WHICH: IF DELUSIONS *******RETURN: A FURTHER INJECTION SHOULD BE ADMINISTERED*****IN MANY CASES THIS WILL NOT BE NECESSARY " " " " " " IN NO**CIRCUMSTANCES: HOWEVER: SHOULD THE DRUG BE ADMINISTERED* DAILY FOR MORE THAN 14 DAYS******************

Ryan acknowledges the message and walks to the control room's main 'porthole'. He activates the screen and looks out at space. The holographic illusion is complete.

Space and the distant suns, the tiny points of light so far away. Ryan's brows contract.

He notices trails in the blackness. They appear to be wisps of vapour and yet they are plainly not escaping from the ship. It is something like smoke from an open fire, trailing in the dark.

He passes his hand across his eyes and peers forward again. The trails are still there.

He is alarmed. He casts his mind over the data he has accumulated, hoping to think of something that will account for the vapour.

Could they be left by the ships of another space-travelling race? It must be a possibility.

Meanwhile the wisps continue to rise. There are more and more of them now. They swirl together, break apart and reform.

Ryan, to his horror, begins to hear a faint noise, a kind of buzzing and ringing in his ears. As the noise begins the gases begin to unite, to shape themselves. Once again Ryan passes a hand over his eyes.

The noises in his ears continue. As he looks out of the porthole once more a terrible suspicion comes over him.

And instantly, staring at him gravely, with a small, malicious smile on her lips, is the old woman. Her eyes are shielded by the round dark glasses. She is black-lipped, her old skin covered in powder. She puts the clawlike hand to the window and is gone.

Ryan gasps and is about to turn from the window in panic when he sees the shapes ahead of him. Out there in space are the whirling figures of his nightmare, the figures of the insane dancers in the darkened ballroom.

They are far away.

Ryan hears their music in his ears. As they dance, slowly and proudly, to the distant chant he watches, paralysed, as they come closer to the ship.

He sees their stiff bodies, their plump, respectable faces, the expensive dark brocades of the women's dresses, the good dark suits of the men. He observes the well-nurtured upright bodies, the straight backs, the air of dignity and comportment with which they circle, so correctly, in time to the music.

The dark circles which are their eyes stare blindly at each other. Their faces are rigid below the dark glasses. They circle through the void towards Ryan and the music becomes louder, more solemn, more threatening.

'Daddy! Daddy!'

Alexander is crying.

Ryan is unable to move. Cold light falls on the dancers. They come closer to the ship, closer to Ryan, standing terrified at his window.

'DADDY!'

Ryan hears the insistent voice and frowns. Is Alex really up?

Ryan smiles. The boy was never one to stay in bed if he could help it.

But Alexander Ryan is not in bed. He is in hibernation.

The dancers dance on.

They are not real. Ryan realises that he should give his attention to his son, not to the illusory dancers out there in space. They can't get in. They can't confront him. They can't take off, in one terrible gesture, the glasses which encircle their eyes, revealing . . .

'GET BACK TO BED ALEX!'

They are very close now. The music slows. They are just a few paces from the ship. They turn to face Ryan with their blinded eyes. Slowly they take a step.

One step . . .

Two steps . . .

Three steps towards Ryan.

They are clustered, some thirty of them, a foot from Ryan, standing just outside the window. And then Ryan realises with greater terror that it has been an illusion. The dancers were not outside. What he was seeing was a reflection in the window. The dancers are actually *behind* him. They have been in the ship all the time. He dare not turn. He stares instead into the mirror.

They stare back.

Then Ryan sees the other. Behind the crowd of dancers are his friends and relatives. All stare at him from blank eyes. All stare at him as if they do not know him. As if, indeed, he does not exist for them.

Josephine — her plump face expressionless, her blonde hair tumbling to her plump shoulders, cruel in her indifference.

His two sons, Alexander and Rupert, startled expressions in their round eyes. Uncle Sidney, his stringing arm gripping the two boys round their thin shoulders, his lips drawn back in a snarl, his eyes on an object somewhere above Ryan's head.

There are the Henry twins, one healthy, one tired by pregnancy, but hand in hand and staring through Ryan with identical hazel eyes. There is Tracy Masterson, looking vacuously past Ryan's left shoulder. There is Fred Masterson, Ryan's oldest friend, a sympathetic expression on his face. There is brother John, puzzled, tired, uncomprehending. There is Isabel, looking bitterly at John.

There is James Henry, red hair gleaming in the mirror-light, glaring meaninglessly through Ryan.

And as he looks, Ryan sees the dancers in front take their last step towards him. He wheels to face them.

He stares into the cool, orderly control room. The screens, the dials, the indicators, the instruments, the computer console. Grey and green, muted colours, quite . . .

He looks back at the porthole. There is only blackness.

In one way this seems worse to Ryan. He begins to beat at the porthole, howling and cursing.

'Where are you? Where are you? You shits, you cunts, you bastards, you bleeders, you fuckers, you horrors . . .'

They are there again. Not the dancers. Only his friends and relatives. But they still cannot see him.

He waves to them, mouths friendly words at them. They do not understand. They come a little closer.

And suddenly Ryan feels their malice, is shocked and horrified. He looks at them and his expression is puzzled. He tries to signal to them — that they know him, that he is their friend.

They crowd closer.

'*Let us in!*' they cry. 'Let us in. Let us in. Let us in. Let us in. Let us in. Let us in. Let us in.'

The clamour around the ship increases. Hands claw at the window. Hands tear their way through the fabric of the porthole.

'You fools! You'll destroy the ship. Be sensible. Wait!' Ryan begs them. 'You'll bring the deaths of all of us! Don't — don't — don't!'

But they are ripping the whole of the wall away, exposing it to frigid space.

'You'll wreck the expedition! Stop it!'

They cannot hear him.

His throat is tight.

He faints.

CHAPTER SIXTEEN

Ryan is lying on the floor of the control room. His sleeve is rolled up and an ampoule of ICC Proditol lies near him. The ampoule is empty.

He blinks. At some point he must have realised what he had to do to stop the hallucinations. He is impressed by his own strength of will.

'How are you now?'

He knows the voice. He feels fear, then relief. It is his brother John's voice. He looks up. His jacket has been folded under his head.

John, stalwart and stolid, looks down at him.

'You *were* in a bad way, old son!'

'John. How did you wake up?'

'Something to do with the computer, I think. There's probably an emergency waking system if anything happens to the man on duty.'

'I'm glad of that. I was a real idiot to carry on on my own. I realised everything else about my condition except the extent of the strain. I was insisting to myself that I didn't need anyone else to help me.'

'Well, you're okay now. I'll help you. You can go into hibernation if you like . . . ?'

'No, that won't be necessary,' Ryan says hastily. 'I'll be able to manage now I've got someone to share my troubles with.' He laughs feebly. 'It's just plain old-fashioned loneliness.' He shudders. He still thinks he can see things in the corners of his eyes. 'I hope.'

'Of course,' says John. He is convinced, he isn't just trying to humour Ryan. John was always a hard man to convince, therefore Ryan is satisfied.

'Thank God for the emergency system, eh?' says John a trifle awkwardly.

'Amen to that,' says Ryan.

He wishes the emergency system had awakened that other member of John's family his young wife Janet. If someone had to be awake . . . He dismisses the thought and gets up. Being with John is almost like being alone, he thinks, for John is not the most voluble of men. Still . . .

Ryan gets up. John is efficiently checking the instruments.

'You'd better get off to your bed, old chap,' says John. 'I'll look after things here.'

Gratefully Ryan goes to his cabin.

*

He lies in the dark, grateful for the drug which has driven away his visions, slightly nervous of the fact that John has joined him.

John probably knows about the affair he had with Janet, John's younger wife. Perhaps he doesn't care.

Then again, perhaps he does. John isn't a particularly vengeful man, but it would be just as well to be on guard.

Ryan remembers the other affair he had. The affair with Sarah Carson — old Carson's daughter . . .

*

Carson's toy business had been Ryan's closest competitor. Carson was Chairman of Moonbeam Toys and had known Ryan for years. They had both started off with Saunders Toys in the old days and had been running pretty much neck and neck ever since. Their rivalry had been a friendly one and they often met for lunch or dinner before the habit of communal eating became unfashionable. When that happened they would still converse over the video.

Carson became a fanatical Patriot one day and, as far as Ryan was concerned, no longer worth speaking to. But by this time it was evident that the Patriots were by far the most powerful political group in the country and Ryan decided it would do him no harm to be Carson's friend. He even attended some meetings with Carson and other Patriots, registering himself as a member.

It was at one of these meetings that he met Sarah, a tall beautiful girl of twenty-two, who did not seem particularly convinced by her father's views.

Josephine was going through a particularly bad time, as were the two boys. All three of them spent two-thirds of the day under sedation and Ryan himself, though he sympathised with their problems, needed some form of relaxation.

The form of relaxation he chose was Sarah Carson. Or, rather, she chose him. The moment she saw him, she made a heavy play for him.

They took to meeting at an all but finished hotel. For a few shillings they could hire a whole suite. The bottom had dropped out of the hotel business by that time. Very few people trusted hotels or liked to leave home.

Sarah pulled Ryan out of his depression and gave him something to look forward to at night. She was passionate and she had stamina. Ryan took to sleeping during the day.

Ryan used the Patriot meetings as an excuse and continued, with Sarah and her father, to turn up at several.

Then Carson had an argument with the rest of his group. Carson had lately formed the opinion that the Earth, far from being a planet circling through space, was in fact a hollowed out 'bubble' in an infinity of rock. Instead of walking about on the outside of a

93

sphere, we were walking about on the inside of one.

Carson went off to form his own group and soon had a healthy following who shared the Hollow Earth belief with him. Sarah continued to go with her father to his meetings (she knew he had a weak heart and also acted, sometimes, as his chauffeur).

Then Carson formed the impression that Ryan was an enemy. Sarah told Ryan this.

'It's the old story — if you're not with me, you're against me. He's getting a bit funny lately,' she said. 'I'm worried about his heart.' She stroked Ryan's chest as they lay together in the hotel bed. 'He's told me to stop seeing you, darling.'

'Are you going to?'

'I think so.'

'Just to humour him? He's eligible for a nut-house now, you know. Even the bloody Patriot fanatics think he's barmy.'

'He's my old dad,' she said. 'I love him.'

'You're hung up on him, if you ask me.'

'Darling, I wouldn't have gone for you if I didn't have a hefty father complex, would I?'

Ryan felt anger. Stupid old fool, Carson! And now his daughter trying to put him down.

'That was clever,' he said bitterly. 'I didn't know you had such sharp knives in your arsenal.'

'Come off it, darling. You brought it up. Anyway, I was only joking. You're not at all bad for your age.'

'Thanks.'

He got up, scowling.

He put a glass under the tap in the wash-basin and filled it with water. He sipped the water gingerly and then threw it down the sink. 'Christ. I'm sure they're putting something in the water, these days.'

'Haven't you heard?' She stretched out in the bed. Her body was near-perfect. She seemed to be taunting him with it. 'There's everything in the water — LSD, cyanide, stuff to rot your brain — you name it!'

He grunted. 'Sure. I think it's probably just dead rats . . .' He got his shirt and began to put it on. 'It's time we were going. It's nine o'clock. The curfew starts at ten.'

'You don't want one last fuck. For old time's sake?'

'You mean it then. About not seeing each other again.'

'I mean it, darling. Make no mistake. The condition he's in, it would kill him . . .'

'He'd be better off dead.'

94

'That's as may be.' She swung her long legs off the bed and began to dress. 'Will you give me a lift home?'

'For old time's sake . . .'

The mixture of rage and depression was getting on top of him. He tried to shrug it off, but it got worse. With all his business worries — production falling, custom declining, debts unpaid — he didn't need this. He knew there was no chance of her changing her mind. She was a direct girl. Her pass at him had been direct. Now the brush-off was direct. He hadn't realised how much she had been bolstering his ego. It was ridiculous to rely on something like that. But he had been. His feelings now told him so.

They left the hotel. The sun was red in the sky. His car was in the street outside. The curfew seemed pretty pointless, for there was hardly anyone in Oxford Street at all.

Ryan stood by the car looking at the ruins of the burnt-out department stores, the gutted office blocks, mementos of the Winter Riots.

Sarah Carson looked out of the window. 'Admiring the view,' she said. 'You're a bit of a romantic on the quiet, aren't you?'

'I suppose I am,' he said as he climbed into the car and started the engine. 'Though I've always considered myself a realist.'

'Just a selfish romantic.'

'You're making it harder than you need to,' he said as he took the car down the street.

'Sorry. I'm not much of a sentimentalist. You can't afford to be, these days.'

'You want me to take you all the way back to Croydon?'

'You don't expect me to *walk* through the Antifem zone, do you?'

'Zone? Have they got control of a whole area now?'

'All but. They're trying to set up their own little state in Balham — allowing no women in at all. Any woman they catch, they kill. Lovely.'

Ryan sniffed. 'They might have the right bloody attitude.'

'Don't get morbid, sweetie. Can we go round Balham?'

'It's the quickest route since the Brighton Road got blown to bits in Brixton.'

'Try going round the other side, then.'

'I'll see.'

They drove for a while in silence.

London was bleak, blackened and broken.

'Ever thought of getting out?' Sarah said as he drove down Vauxhall Bridge Road, trying to avoid the potholes. He had begun to feel slightly sick. Partly her, he thought, and partly the damned agorophobia.

'Where is there to go?' he said. 'The rest of the world seems to be worse off than England.'

'Sure.'

'And you need money to live abroad,' he said. 'Since nobody recognises anyone else's currency any more, what would I live on?'

'You think people are going to buy a lot of toys this Christmas?' She was looking at the completely flattened houses on the right.

His depression and his anger grew. He shrugged. He knew she was right.

'You and my old dad are in the wrong business,' she said cheerfully. 'At least he had the sense to go into politics. That's a bit more secure — for a while, at any rate.'

'Maybe.' He drove over the bridge. It shook as he crossed.

'A strong wind'll finish that,' she said.

'Shut up, Sarah.' He gripped the wheel hard.

'Oh God. Try to finish this thing off gracefully, darling. I thought you were such a good business man. Such a cunning bastard. Such a cool bird, working out all the odds. That's what you told me.'

'No need to throw it in my face. I've got plans, my love, that you haven't an inkling of.'

'Not the spaceship idea!' She laughed.

'How — ?'

'You didn't tell me darling. I went through your briefcase a couple of weeks ago. Are you really serious? You're not going to take thirteen people to Siberia and steal that U.N. spaceship that's been standing idle for the last year.'

'It's ready to go.'

'They're still bickering over who owns what bit of it and whose nationals have got a right to go in it. It'll never take off.'

Ryan smiled secretly.

'You're nuttier than my old man, sweetie!'

Ryan scowled.

'Wait till I tell my friends,' she said. 'I'll be dining out on it for weeks.'

'You'd better not tell anyone, my love,' He spoke through his teeth. 'I mean it.'

'Come *on*, darling. We all have our illusions, but this is ridiculous. How would you fly one of those things?'

'It's fully automatic,' he said. 'It's the most sophisticated piece of machinery ever invented.'

'And you think they're going to let you pinch it?'

'We're already in touch with the people at the station,' he said. 'They seem to agree we can do it.'

'How are you in touch with them?'

'It's not hard, Sarah. Old-fashioned radio. For some time a few scientifically minded pragmatists like myself have been working towards a way of getting out of this mess, since it seems impossible to save the human race from sinking back to the Dark Ages . . ."

'You could have saved it once,' Sarah said, turning to look directly at him. 'If you hadn't been so bloody careful. So bloody selfish!'

'It wasn't as simple as that.'

'Your generation and the generation before that could have done something. The seeds of all this ridiculous paranoia and xenophobia were there then. God — such a waste! This century could have been a century of Utopia. You and your mothers and fathers turned it into Hell.'

'It might look like that . . .'

'Darling, it *was* like that.'

He shrugged.

'And now you're getting out,' she said. 'Leaving the mess behind. Your talk of "pragmatism" is so much bloody balls! You're as much an escaper as my poor daft old dad! Maybe more of one — and less pleasant, for that — because you might fucking succeed!'

They were driving through Stockwell. The sun was setting but no street lighting came on.

'You feel guilty because you're letting me down, don't you?' he said. 'That's what all this display is about, isn't it?'

'No. You're a good fuck. But I never cared much for your character, darling.'

'You'll have to go a long way to find a better one in these dark days.' He tried to say it as a joke, but it was evident he believed it.

'Selfish and opinionated,' she said. 'Pragmatism. Ugh!'

'I'll drop you off here then, shall I?'

He stopped the car. It sank on its cushion of air.

She peered out into the darkness. 'Where's "here"?'

'Balham,' he said.

'Don't play games, darling. Let's get this over with. You were taking me all the way to Croydon, remember.'

'I'm a bit tired of your small-talk — darling.'

'All right.' She leaned back. 'I'll button my lip, I promise. I'll say nothing until we get to Croydon and then I'll give you a sweet "thank you".'

But he had made his decision. It wasn't malice. It was self-preservation. It was for Josephine and the boys, and for the group. He wasn't enjoying what he was doing.

'Get out of the car, Sarah.'

'You take me bloody home the way you said you would!'

'Out.'

She looked into his eyes. 'My God, Ryan . . .'

'Go on.' He pushed her shoulder, leaned over her and opened the door. 'Go on.'

'Jesus Christ. All right.' She picked up her handbag from the seat and got out of the car. 'It's something of a classic situation. But a bit too classic really. The sex war's hotted up in this part of the world.'

'That's your problem,' he said.

'I'm not likely to get out of this alive, Ryan.'

'That's your problem.'

She took a deep breath. 'I won't tell anyone about your stupid spaceship idea, if that's what's worrying you. Who'd believe me, anyway?'

'I've got a family and friends to worry about, Sarah. They believe me.'

'You dirty shit.' She walked off into the darkness.

They must have been waiting for her all the time because she screamed — a high-pitched, ugly scream — she cried out for him to help her. Her second scream was cut short.

Ryan closed the door of the car and locked it. He started the engine and switched on the headlights.

He saw her face in the lights. It stuck out above the black mass of Antifems in their monklike robes.

It was only her face.

Her body lay on the ground, still clasping her handbag.

Her head was on the end of the pole.

CHAPTER SEVENTEEN

Ryan lies in his bunk with his log-book and his stylus. He has been there for two days now. John comes in occasionally, but doesn't bother him, realising that he does not want to be disturbed. He lets Ryan get his own food when he wants to and looks after the running of the ship. To make sure that Ryan rests, he has even turned off the console in Ryan's cabin.

Ryan spends most of his time with the log-book. He removed it from the desk originally to make sure that John didn't come across it.

He reads over the first entry he made when he brought it back to the cabin.

What I did to Sarah can be justified, of course, in that she could have ruined this project. I had to be sure nothing wrecked it. The fact that we are all safe and aboard is evidence that I took the right precautions — trusting no one outside the group — making sure that everything was done with the utmost secrecy. We kept contact only with the Russian group — about the last outpost of rational humanity that we knew about.

Would I have done it in that way if she had not turned me down in such an unpleasant manner? I don't know. Considering the state of things at the time, I behaved no worse, no less humanely, than anyone else. You had to fight fire with fire. And if it — and certain other things — is on my conscience, at least it isn't on anyone else's conscience. The boys are clean. So is Josephine. So are most of the others . . .

He sighs as he reads the entry over. He shifts his body in the bunk.

'All right, old chap?'

John has come, as silently as ever, into the cabin. He looks a trifle tired himself.

'I'm fine.' Ryan closes the book quickly. 'Fine. Are you all right?'

'I'm coping very well. I'll let you know if anything crops up.'

'Thanks.'

John leaves. Ryan returns his attention to the log, turning the pages until he comes to a fresh one.

He continues writing:

There is no doubt about it. I have blood on my hands. That's probably the reason I've been having bad dreams. Any normal, half-way decent man would. I took it on myself to do, at least. I didn't involve anyone else.

When we hijacked the Albion transport, I had hoped there would be no trouble. Neither would there have been, I think, if the crew had been all English. Incredible! I always knew the Irish were excitable, but that stupid fellow who tried to get the gun from me in mid-air deserved all he got. He must have been Irish. There's no other explanation. I was never a racialist, but one had to admit that there were certain virtues the English have which other races don't share. I suppose that is racialism of a sort. But not the unhealthy sort. I was horrified when I heard that the foreigners in the camps were being starved to death. I would have done something about it if

99

I could. But by that time it had gone too far. Maybe Sarah was right. Maybe I could have stopped it if I hadn't been so selfish. I always considered myself to be an enlightened man — a liberal man. I was known for it.

He stops again, staring at the wall.

The rot had set in before my day. H-bombs, nuclear radiation, chemical poisoning, insufficient birth control, mismanaged economics, misguided political theories. And then — panic.

And no room for error. Throw a spanner in the works of a society as sophisticated and highly tuned as ours was and — that's it. Chaos.

They tried to bring simple answers to complicated problems. They looked for messiahs when they should have been looking at the problems. Humanity's old trouble. But this time humanity did for itself. Absolutely.

It is odd, he thinks, that I will never know how it all turned out. Just as well, of course, from the point of view of our kids. We left just in time. They were bombing each other to smithereens . . .

Another few days, he writes, *and we wouldn't have made it. I timed it pretty well, all things considered.*

*

Ryan had led the party out to London Airport where the big Albion transport was preparing to take off on its bombing mission over Dublin. They were all in military kit for Ryan was posing as a general with his staff.

They had driven straight out on to the runway and were up the steps and into the plane before anyone knew what had happened.

At gunpoint Ryan had told the pilot to take off.

Within quarter of an hour they were heading for Russia . . .

It had been over the landing strip on the bleak Siberian Plain that the Irishman — he must have been an Irishman — had panicked. How an Irishman had managed to remain under cover without revealing his evident racial characteristics, Ryan would never know.

For two hours Ryan had sat in the co-pilot's seat with his Purdy automatic trained on the pilot while Henry and Masterson looked after the rest of the crew and John Ryan and Uncle Sidney stayed with the families.

Ryan was tired. He felt drained of energy. His body ached and the butt of the gun was slippery with the sweat from his hands. He felt filthy and his flesh was cold. As the Albion came down through the clouds he saw the huge spaceship standing on the launching field. It was surrounded by webs of gantries, like a caged bird of prey, like Prometheus bound.

His attention was on the ship when the Irish pilot leapt from his seat.

'You damned traitor! You disgusting renegade . . .' The pilot lunged for the gun, screaming at the top of his voice, his face writhing with his hatred and his insanity.

Ryan fell back, pressing the trigger. The Purdy muttered and a stream of tiny explosive bullets hit the pilot all over his chest and face and his bloody body collapsed on top of Ryan.

Pilotless, the big transport began to shake.

Ryan pushed the body off him and reached up to throw the lever that would put the plane automatically on Emergency Landing Procedure. The plane's rockets fired and the transport juddered as its trajectory was arrested. It began to go down vertically on its rockets.

Ryan wiped the sweat from his lip and then retched. He had smeared the pilot's blood all over his mouth. He cleaned his face with his sleeve, watching as the plane neared the ground, screaming towards the overgrown airstrip to the north of the launching field.

John Ryan put his head into the cabin 'My God! What happened?'

'The pilot just went mad,' Ryan said hoarsely. 'You'd better check everyone's got their safety belts on, John. We're going to make a heavy landing.'

The Albion was close to the ground now, its rockets burning the concrete strip. Ryan buckled his own safety belt.

Five feet above the ground the rockets cut out and the plane belly-flopped on to the concrete.

Shaken, Ryan got out of his seat and stumbled into the crew section. Alexander was crying and Tracey Masterson was screaming and Ida Henry was moaning, but the rest were very quiet.

'John,' Ryan said. 'Get the doors open and get everybody out of the plane as soon as possible will you?' He still held the Purdy.

John Ryan nodded and Ryan went aft to where Masterson and Henry were covering the rest of the crew.

'What was all that about?' James Henry said suspiciously. 'You trying to kill us all, Ryan?'

'The pilot lost his head. We had to make an emergency rocket-powered landing — vertical.' Ryan looked over the rest of the crew — four boys and a woman of about thirty. They all looked scared. 'Did you know your captain was Irish?' Ryan asked them. 'And you were going to bomb Dublin? You can bet your life he was going to try and make a landing.'

The crew stared at him incredulously.

'Well, it was true,' Ryan said. 'But don't worry. I've dealt with him.'

The woman said: 'You murdered him. Is that what you did?'

'Self-defence,' said Ryan. 'Self-defence isn't murder. All right, Fred — Henry — you go and help everybody get off this bloody plane.'

The woman said: 'He was no more Irish than I am. Anyway, what does it matter?'

'No wonder your people are losing,' Ryan answered contemptuously.

When everyone was off the ship Ryan shot the crew. It was the only safe thing to do. While they were alive there was a chance that they would seize control of the Albion and do something foolish.

*

Tishchenko was a harried-looking man of about fifty. He gravely shook hands with Ryan and then guided him by the elbow across the barren concrete towards the control buildings. The wind was cold and moaned. Beyond the launching site, the plain stretched in all directions, featureless and green-grey. Ryan's people trudged behind them.

Tishchenko was the man whom Ryan had contacted originally. The contact had been made through Allard who had been one of the people vainly trying to keep the U.N. together in the last days. Allard, an old school-friend of Ryan's, had been sent to a Patriot camp not long after he had put Ryan in touch with Tishchenko.

'It is a great pleasure,' said Tishchenko as they entered the building that had been converted to living quarters. It was cold and gloomy. 'And something of an achievement that, in the midst of all this insane xenophobia, a little international group of sane men and women can work together on a project as important as this one.' He smiled. 'And it's good to be able to look at a woman again, I can tell you.'

Ryan was tired. He nodded, rubbing his eyes. One of the reasons the Russian group had been so eager to deal with his group was because of the number of women he could bring with him.

'You are weary?' Tishchenko said. 'Come.'

He led them up two flights of stairs and showed them their accommodation. Camp beds had been lined around the walls of three rooms. 'It is about the best we can provide,' Tishchenko apologised. 'Amenities are few. Everything had to go to the ship.'

He went to the window and drew back the blankets that covered it. 'There she is.'

They gathered around the window and looked at the spacecraft. She towered into the sky.

'She has been ready to fly for two years.' Tishchenko shook his head. 'It has taken two years to provision her. The civil war here, and then the Chinese invasion, is what protected us. We were all but forgotten about . . .'

'Who else is here now?' Ryan asked. 'Just Russians?'

Tishchenko smiled. 'Just two Russians — myself and Lipche. A couple of Americans, a Chinese, two Italians, three Germans, a Frenchman. That's it.'

Ryan drew a deep breath. He felt odd. The shock of the killings, he supposed.

'I'll be back in a few minutes to take you down to dinner,' Tishchenko told him.

Ryan looked up. 'What?'

'Dinner. We all eat together on the floor below.'

'Oh, I see . . .'

'I couldn't,' said Josephine Ryan. 'I really couldn't . . .'

'We're not used to it, you see,' said James Henry. 'Our customs — well . . .'

Tishchenko looked puzzled and very slightly perturbed. 'Well, if you'd like to arrange to bring the food up here, I suppose we can do that . . . Then perhaps we can meet after meals. You have been in the thick of things, of course. We have been isolated. We haven't really experienced . . .'

'Yes,' said Ryan, 'it has been very nasty. I'm sorry. Some of our social sicknesses have rather rubbed off on us. Give us a day or two to settle. We'll be all right then, I'm sure.'

'Good,' said Tishchenko.

Ryan watched him leave. He sensed a certain antipathy in the Russian's manner. He hoped there would not be trouble with him. Russians could not always be trusted. For one moment he wondered if they had been led into a complicated trap. Could this team of scientists just be after the women? Would they dispense with the men now that they had served their purpose?

Ryan pulled himself together. An irrational idea. He would have to watch himself more carefully. He had had no sleep for two nights. Get some rest now, he told himself, and you'll be your old self in the morning.

*

The thirteen English people and the eleven scientists toured the ship.

'It is all completely automatic,' said Schonberg, one of the Germans. He smiled and patted Alexander on the head. 'A child could run it.'

The English party, rested and more relaxed, were in better spirits. Even James Henry, who had been the most suspicious of all, seemed better.

'And your probes proved conclusively that there are two planets in the system capable of supporting human life,' he said to Boulez, the Frenchman.

The French scientist smiled. 'One of them could be Earth. About the same amount of land and sea, very similar ecology. There was bound to be a planet like it somewhere — we were just lucky to discover one this early.'

Buccella, one of the Italians, was taking a strong interest in pointing out certain features of the ship to Janet Ryan.

Typical Italian, thought Ryan.

He glanced at his brother John who was listening carefully as Shan, the Chinese, tried to explain about the regeneration units. Shan's English was not very good.

*

Back in their own quarters, Ryan asked his brother: 'Did you notice that Italian, Buccella, and Janet together?'

'What do you mean "together"?' John said with a grin.

Ryan shrugged. 'It's your problem.'

The preparations continued swiftly. News came in of massive nuclear bombardments taking place all over the globe. They took to working night and day, resting when they could no longer keep their eyes open. And at length the ship was ready.

Buccella, Shan and Boulez were going on the ship with the others. The rest were staying behind. Their job was to get the ship off the ground. They were taking over the duties of some fifty technicians.

Lift-off day arrived.

CHAPTER EIGHTEEN

Ryan scratches his nose with the tip of his stylus. He writes:
One could not afford to be sentimental in those days. Perhaps when we land on the new planet we can relax and indulge all those pleasant human vices. It would be nice to feel at peace again, the way one did as a child.

He shifts in his bunk and looks up.

'Good God, Janet. You're up!'

Janet Ryan smiles down at him. 'We're all up. John thought it wisest.'

'I suppose he knows what he's doing. It's not part of the original plan.'

'John wants to see how it works out. Can I get you anything?'

He grins. 'No thanks, love. I've got my Proditol to keep me cool. It seems to be working fine. I've been doing some pretty sober thinking since I decided to stay in bed for a bit.'

'John says you'd got pretty obsessive — were following ship routine to the point of your own breakdown . . .'

'I can see I was half crazy now. I'm very well — very relaxed.'

'You'll soon be in control of things again,' she smiles.

'I certainly will!'

Janet leaves the cabin.

Ryan writes:

Janet has just been in to see me. Apparently brother John feels it's best for everybody to be up and about. I expect Josephine and the boys will be along soon. Janet looks as beautiful as ever. You couldn't really blame that Italian chap for going overboard for her . . . A sick joke that, I suppose. When I caught him with her in John's own cabin, I felt sick. The man was a complete stinker, playing around like that. He had to be dealt with. His friends had their eyes on the girls, too, that was plain. They were only waiting for a chance to get their hands on them while our backs were turned. I was a fool to trust a pack of foreigners. I know that now.

It became evident that his friends were in on the plot with him, the way they took his part. They threatened the security of the whole mission with their utterly irrational intentions on the girls — and the boys, too, I shouldn't wonder. I suppose it was that they hadn't seen any women for so long. It went to their heads. They couldn't control themselves. In a way one can sympathise, of course. It showed just what a threat to the safety of the ship they were when they tried to steal my gun. I had to shoot Buccella then and his friends, when they wouldn't stop coming at me. We pushed the corpses through the airlock. Everybody agreed I had done the right thing.

He sighs. It has been hard, keeping control of everything for so long. Making unpleasant decisions . . .

Strange that Josephine and the boys haven't come in, yet. John is probably staging the wake-up procedure.

He closes the log and puts it and the stylus under his pillow. He leans back, looking forward to seeing his wife and children.

He dozes.

He sleeps.

He dreams.

*

Q: WHO ARE YOU KIDDING?
A: HAD A NOISE TROUBLE

*

He stands in the control room. He is sure he has forgotten something, some crucial operation. He checks the computer, but it is babbling nonsense. Puns and facetious remarks flow from it. He casts around for the source of the trouble, looks for a way to switch off the computer. But it will not switch off. The life of the ship depends on the computer. But it is the ship or Ryan, as Ryan sees it. He starts to batter at the computer with a chair.
******YOURE KILLING ME**********HAHAHAHAHA HA**
says the computer.

Ryan turns. Through the porthole he sees the dancers again, their faces pressed against the glass.

'You're in league with them,' he tells the computer. 'You're on their side.'
*******I AM ON EVERYONES SIDE***********I AM A** SCIENTIFIC INSTRUMENT******I AM UTTERLY PRAG-MATIC**
says the computer.

'You're laughing at me now,' Ryan says almost pathetically. 'You're taking a rise out of me, aren't you?'
*******MY DUTY IS TO LOOK AFTER YOU ALL AND KEEP YOU SAFE AND SOUND""""""""REPEAT SAFE AND SOUND**

'You cynical bugger.'

He sees a sweet old lady shaking her head, a wry smile on her face. 'Language,' she says. 'Language.'

It is his mother. Her maiden name was Hope Dempsey. He christened the ship after her.

'You tell the computer to stop getting at me, ma!' he begs.

'Naughty thing,' says his mother. 'You leave my little boy alone.'

But the computer continues to mock him.

'You were never a sweet old lady anyway,' says Ryan. She turns into the hag who haunts him and he screams.

*

Josephine stands over him. She is holding an empty ampoule of Proditol. 'You'll feel better in a moment, darling,' she says. 'How are you now?'

'Better already,' he says, smiling in relief. 'You don't know how pleased I am to see you, Jo. Where are the boys?'

'They're not quite awake yet. You know it takes a bit of time.' She sits on the edge of his bunk. 'They'll be here soon. You should have woken us up earlier, you know. It's too much of a strain for one man — even you.'

'I realise that now,' he says.

She gives the old slightly nervous, slightly tender smile. 'Take it easy,' she says. 'Let the Proditol do its stuff.'

She catches sight of the red log-book sticking from under his pillow. 'What's that, darling?'

'My log-book,' he says. 'A sort of private diary, really.'

'If it's private . . .'

'I'd rather keep it that way until I've had a look through it. When I feel better.'

'Of course.'

'It's the only thing that kept me halfway sane,' he explains.

'Of course.'

*

With one hand supporting his head, Ryan lies in his bunk and writes:

Alexander and Rupert both look fit and well and everybody seems singularly cheerful. It seems as if we have all benefited from rest and with breaking ties with Earth. We feel free again. I can hear them bustling about in the ship. Laughter. A general mood of easy co-operation. What a change from the early days on the ship, when even Uncle Sidney seemed jealous of my command! Even sullen, suspicious old James Henry has an almost saintly manner! My morbid thoughts melt like snow in springtime. My obsession for Janet has disappeared — part of the same morbid mood, I suppose. James Henry's new attitude surprises me most. If it wasn't for the fact that everybody is in better spirits I'd suspect that he was once again harbouring plans to get rid of me and run the ship himself. It is amazing what a change of environment can do! John was wise to awaken everybody. Plainly, I had become too worried that the tensions would start up again. We're going to make a fine colony on New Earth. And thank God for Proditol. Those scientists certainly covered every angle. I've decided to put all morbid thoughts of the past out of my mind. I was a different person — perhaps a sick person — when I did what I did. To indulge in self-recrimination now is stupid and benefits nobody.

My breakdown was caused by the chaos that crept over society. It reflected the breakdown of that society. I could almost date its beginning for me — when our own air force (or, at least, what had been our own air force) dropped napalm and fragmentation bombs on London. My psyche, I suppose, reflected the environment.

But enough of that! I've made up my mind. No more morbid self-examination. No need for it now, anyway.

The days will pass more quickly now that everybody is up and about and so cheerful. We'll be landing on that planet before we realise it!

He signs the page, closes the book and tucks it under his pillow. He feels a little weak. Doubtless the effects of the drug. He sleeps and dreams that the ship has landed on the Isle of Skye and everyone is swimming in the sea. He watches them all swim out. James Henry, Janet Ryan, Josephine Ryan, Rupert Ryan, Sidney Ryan, Fred Masterson, Alexander Ryan, Ida and Felicity Henry, Tracy Masterson. Isabel Ryan. They are laughing and shouting. They all swim out into the sea.

*

A week passes.

Ryan spends less time writing in his log book and more time sleeping. He feels confident that John and the others are running the ship well.

One night he is awakened by pangs of hunger and he realises that nobody has thought to bring him any food. He frowns. An image of the Foreigners comes into his mind. He saw a camp only once, but it was enough. They were not being gassed or burned or shot — they were being systematically starved to death. The cheapest way. His stomach rumbles.

He gets up and leaves his cabin. He enters the storeroom and takes a meal pack from a bin. Chewing at the pack, he pads back to his cabin.

He has a slight headache — probably the effects of the Proditol. They have given him a dose every day for the past ten days or so. It will be time to finish the doses soon.

He sleeps.

CHAPTER NINETEEN

Ryan makes an entry in his log:

I have now been resting for two weeks and the difference is amazing. I have lost weight — I was too heavy anyway — and my brain has cleared. I have had insights into my own behaviour (amazing what a clever rationaliser I am!) and my body is relaxed. I will soon be ready to resume control of the ship.

Josephine enters. She is holding an ampoule of Proditol in her hand.

'Time for your shot, dear,' she smiles.

'Hey! What are you trying to do to me.' He grins at her. 'Fourteen days is the maximum period for that stuff. I don't need it any more.'

Her smile fades. 'One more shot can't do you any harm, dear, can it?'

He swings himself out of the bunk. 'What's up?' he jokes. 'Is there something you don't want me to know about?'

'Of course not!'

Ryan unfolds a suit from the pack in the cupboard. He lays it on the bed. 'I'm going to take a shower,' he says. 'Then I'll go into the control room and see how everyone's getting along without me.'

'You're not well enough yet, dear,' says Josephine, her pink face anxious. 'Please stay in bed a bit longer, even if you won't let me give you the Proditol.'

'I'm fine.' Ryan frowns. He feels a return of his old feelings of suspicion. Maybe he should have something more to keep him calm — yet if he has any more Proditol, he exceeds the dose and risks his life. 'I'd like to stay in my bunk all the time,' he smiles. 'Honest, I would. But the suggested dosage period is over, Jo. I've got to get up sometime.'

He leaves the cabin and takes his shower. He comes back in.

Josephine has gone. She has laid out a fresh disposable suit on the bed. He puts it on.

He walks along the passage towards the main control room and he remembers that he has left his diary under his pillow. There is a chance that someone will give in to the temptation to read it. It would be better if no one saw his comments. After all, some of them were pretty insane. Some of it is a bit like a prisoner of the Inquisition, confessing to anything that is suggested to him!

He smiles and returns to his cabin. He picks up the log-book and puts it in his locker, sealing the locker.

He still feels weak. He sits on the edge of the bunk for a moment.

For some time now he has been aware of a sound. Now it impinges on his consciousness. A high-pitched whine. He recognises the noise. An emergency in the control room.

He gets up and runs out of his cabin, down the passage, into the main control room.

The computer is flashing a sign:

URGENT ATTENTION REQUIRED
URGENT ATTENTION REQUIRED

James Henry is at the control. He turns as Ryan enters. 'Hello, Ryan. How are you now?'

'I'm fine. What's the emergency?'

'Nothing much. I'm coping with it.'

'What is it, though?'

'A new circuit needed in the heat control unit in the hydroponics section. Cut out the emergency signal would you?'

Ryan automatically does as Henry asks him.

Henry makes a few adjustments to the controls then turns to Ryan with a smile. 'Glad to see you're okay again. I've been managing pretty well in your absence.'

'That's great . . .' Ryan feels a touch of anger at Henry's slightly patronising tone.

Ryan looks around the control room. Everything else seems to be as he left it at the time of his breakdown. 'Where's everybody else?' he asks.

'Studying — resting — checking out various functions — standard ship routine.'

'You seem to be working together very well,' Ryan says.

'Better than before. We've got something in common now, after all.'

Ryan feels a touch of panic. He doesn't know why. Is there something in Henry's tone? A sort of triumph? 'What do you mean?'

Henry shrugs. 'Our great mission.'

'Of course,' says Ryan. He sucks his lower lip. 'Of course.'

But what did James Henry really mean? Is it that they have got rid of him. Do they believe that he was the cause of their tension? Is that what Henry is insinuating?

Ryan feels his throat go dry. He feels his anger rising.

He controls himself. He isn't thinking clearly. He still needs to rest. Josephine was right.

'Well, keep up the good work, James,' he says, turning to leave. 'If there's anything I can do . . .'

'You could check the Hibernation Room some time,' Henry says.

'What?' Ryan frowns.

'I said you could check the hydration loom — in hydroponics.'

'Sure. Now?'

'Any time you feel like it.'

'Okay. I'm still a bit shaky. I'll get back to my bunk, I think.'

'I think you'd better.'

'I'm perfectly all right now.'

'Sure. But you could still do with some rest.'

Ryan again controls his temper. 'Yes. Well — I'll see you later.'

'I'm here whenever you need me, captain.'

Again the feeling that James Henry is mocking him, just as he used to, before it became intolerable . . .

He feels faint. No. Henry is right. He's still not properly recovered. He staggers back to his cabin.

He falls into his bunk.

He sleeps and he dreams.

*

He is in the control room again. James Henry stands there. James Henry is trying to supersede him. James Henry has always wished to take over command of the group and of the spaceship. But James Henry is not stable enough to command. If he takes over from Ryan the whole safety of the ship becomes at risk. Ryan knows that there is only one thing to do to stop Henry's plotting against him.

He raises the Purdy automatic — the same gun that he used on the aircraft. He levels it at James Henry. He takes a deep breath and begins to squeeze the trigger.

The computer flashes:

URGENT ATTENTION REQUIRED

URGENT ATTENTION REQUIRED

111

Henry turns. Ryan hides the gun behind his back. Henry signals to him to have a look at the computer. Ryan approaches it suspiciously.

******YOU ARE IN NO CONDITION TO COMMAND THIS******CRAFT"""""""""REPEAT YOU ARE IN NO CONDITION TO******COMMAND THIS CRAFT"""""""""" REPEAT YOU ARE IN NO******CONDITION TO COMMAND THIS CRAFT"""""""""TAKE ONE DOSE*ICC PRODITOL INSTANTLY AND REPEAT DOSE DAILY FOR*** FOURTEEN DAYS"""""""""YOU ARE IN NO CONDITION TO******COMMAND THIS CRAFT"""""""""YOU ARE ENDANGERING THE****ENTIRE EXPEDITION IF YOU DO NOT FOLLOW THESE******INSTRUCTIONS AT ONCE"""""""""REPEAT AT ONCE********************

Ryan looks contemptuously at Henry. 'You'll use anything to try to discredit me, won't you?'

Henry says calmly: 'You are a sick man, Ryan. The computer's right. Why don't you . . . ?'

Ryan raises the Purdy automatic and fires one bullet into Henry's skull. The man's head jerks back. He opens his mouth to say something. Ryan fires again. James Henry falls.

Ryan scowls at the computer. 'The next one's for you if you go on playing games with me, chum.'

He turns the cut-out switch.

*******YOU ARE IN NO CONDITION TO COMMAND THIS**
URGENT ATTENTION REQUIRED
URGENT AT
Tension, tension everywhere
Not any time to think
CRAFT"""""""""REPEAT YOU ARE IN NO CONDITION TO**
There is d . . .
Q. WHAT IS THE EXACT NATURE OF THE CATASTROPHE?

*

Ryan wakes up, sweating. His suit is torn. The bunk is in a mess. He climbs off the bunk and stands on the floor, shaking. The Proditol just hasn't been enough. But he can't risk taking any more. He strips the bunk and disposes of the covers. He takes off his clothes and disposes of them.

A feeling of desperation engulfs him. Is he really incurable?

Will he never shake the nightmares? He was sure he was better. And yet . . .

Suppose they haven't been giving him Proditol. Suppose they are deliberately poisoning him. No. Not his friends. Not his family. They couldn't be so cruel.

And yet hasn't he been cruel? Hasn't he done as much for expediency's sake?

He sobs, drawing in huge breaths.

Ryan falls on his bunk and weeps.

He weeps for a long while before he hears his brother John's voice.

'What's the matter, old chap?'

He looks up. John's face is sympathetic. But can he trust him?

'I'm still getting the nightmares, John. They're just as bad. Worse, if anything.'

John spreads his hands helplessly. 'You must try to rest. Take some sleeping pills. Try to sleep, for God's sake. There's nothing to worry about. The responsibility was too much for you. No one man should have to bear such a burden. You're afraid that you might weaken — but it is right to weaken sometimes. You expect too much of yourself, old son.'

'Yes.' Ryan rubs at his face. 'I've done my best, John. For all of you.'

'Of course.'

'What?'

'Of course you have.'

'People are never grateful.'

'We're grateful, old chap.'

'I'm a murderer, John. I murdered for your sake.'

'You took too much on. It was self-defence.'

'That's what I think, but . . .'

'Try to rest.'

More tears fall from Ryan's eyes.

'I'll try, John.'

*

The music has started again. The drums are beating. Ryan watches the dancers circle about the control room. They are smiling fixed, insincere smiles. James Henry dances with one of them. He has two holes in his forehead.

Ryan wakes up.

*

113

The dream is so vivid that Ryan can hardly believe he did not shoot James Henry. Obviously he didn't. John would have mentioned it. He gets out of his bunk and pulls on a new suit of coveralls. He leaves the cabin and goes to the control room.

It is empty, silent save for the muted noises of the instruments. There is no sign of any sort of struggle.

Ryan smiles at his own stupidity and leaves the control room.

Only when he is back in his bunk does he realise that there should have been someone on watch.

He frowns.

Things are relaxed. But should they be lax?

He feels he should go and check, but he is sleepy . . .

*

He awakes to find the smiling face of his wife Josephine bending over him.

'How are you?'

'Still rough,' he says. 'You were right. I should have stayed in my bunk longer.'

'You'll be fit and well soon.'

He nods, but he is not confident. She seems to understand this.

'Don't worry,' she says softly. 'Don't worry.'

'I suspect everyone, Jo — even you. That's not healthy, is it?'

'Don't worry.'

She goes towards the door. 'Fred Masterson's thinking of dropping in later. Do you want to see him?'

'Old Fred? Sure.'

*

Fred Masterson sat on the edge of Ryan's bunk.

'You're still feeling a bit under the weather, I hear,' Fred said. 'Still got the old persecution stuff, eh?'

Ryan nods. 'I once heard someone say that if you had persecution feelings it usually meant you were being persecuted,' he says. 'Though not always from the source you suspect.'

'That's a bit complicated for me.' Fred laughs. 'You know old Fred — simple-minded.'

Ryan smiles slowly. He is pleased to see Fred.

'I cracked up once,' Fred continues. 'Do you remember? That awful business with Tracy?'

Ryan shakes his head. 'No . . .'

'Come on — you remember. When I thought Tracy was having it off with James Henry. You must remember. When we'd only

114

been on the ship for a month.'

Ryan frowns. 'No. I can't remember. Did you mention it?'

'Mention it! I should think I did! You helped me out of that one. It was you who suggested that Tracy would be better off if she was in hibernation.'

'Oh yes. Yes, I do remember. She was overwrought . . .'

'We all were. We decided that in order to ease the tension she should enter her container a bit earlier than scheduled.'

'That's right. Of course . . .'

'Off course,' says Masterson.

Ryan looks at him. 'You're not — you're not having a joke with me are you, Fred?'

'Why should I do that?'

'I'm still getting a touch of the trouble I had earlier. Visual hallucinations. It's nasty.'

'I bet it is.'

Ryan turns in the bunk. 'I'm a bit tired now, Fred.'

'I'll be off, then. See you. Keep smiling.'

'See you,' says Ryan.

When Masterson has gone, he frowns. He really doesn't remember much about Tracy and Masterson's problems with her.

It begins to dawn on him that he might not be as disturbed as he thinks. If he is in a bad way, might not some of the others be in equally poor shape? Maybe Fred Masterson has a few delusions of his own to contend with?

It is a likely explanation. He had better be careful. And he had better humour Fred next time he sees him.

He begins to worry.

If they are all in bad shape, then that could threaten the smooth running of the ship. It is up to him to get well soon, keep a careful eye on the others.

People under stress do odd things, after all. They get peculiar paranoid notions. Like James Henry's . . .

Next time he sees John, he'll suggest, reasonably, that James Henry have another spell of hibernation. For his own sake and the sake of the rest of them. It could be suggested quite subtly to James.

CHAPTER TWENTY

Ryan's dreams continue.

Once again he is in the control room. Most of his dreams take place in the control room now. He stares through the porthole at the void, at the dancers with their round black glasses, at his friends and family who stand behind the dancers. Sometimes he sees the old woman.

When occasionally he wakes — and it is not now very often — he realises that he must be under heavy sedation.

He hears the music — the high-pitched music — and it makes his flesh crawl. Dimly he wonders what is happening to him, what his one-time friends, his treacherous family are doing to him. There is now no question in his mind that he is the victim of some complicated deception, that he has been victim to this deception perhaps even before the spaceship took off, certainly after it left Earth.

He does not know why they should be working against him, however; particularly since he is the chief engineer of their salvation.

He is too weak, too drugged to do more than speculate about their plans.

Was this why they were all originally put into hibernation?

He seems to remember something about that now. Was that why he was so insistent that they should not be awakened until the end of the journey? Could be.

But he had to crack up temporarily. The ship's emergency system awakened John who awakened the others and now they are in control, they have him in their power.

It is even possible that they are not his family and friends at all, but could have brainwashed him into thinking they are. He remembers that old Patriot rally.

'They look like us, sound like us — in every respect they are human — but they are not human . . .'

God! It couldn't be true!

But what other explanation is there for the strange behaviour of the rest of the personnel on board the *Hope Dempsey*?

Ryan moves restlessly on the bunk. He has cracked up — no doubt about that. And the reason, too, is obvious — strain, over-work, too much responsibility. But there is no such explanation, when he thinks about it, for the behaviour of the others.

The others are mad.

Or they are . . .

... not human.

'No,' he murmurs. 'Not Josephine and the boys. I'd realise it, surely. Not Janet, warm little Janet. Not Uncle Sidney and John and Fred Masterson and the women. And James Henry half believed the Patriots. He couldn't be one. Unless he was so cunning he ...'

He rolls on the bunk.

'No,' he groans. 'No.'

John comes into the cabin. 'What's the matter, old son? What's bothering you now?'

Ryan looks up at him, wanting to trust his brother, wanting to confide in him, but he can't.

'Betray me ...' he mutters. 'You've betrayed me, John.'

'Come off it.' John tries to laugh. 'What would I want to betray you for? How could I betray you? We're on your side. Remember the old days? Us against the world? The only ones who could see the terrible state the world was in. The only ones who had a plan to deal with it. Remember your apartment? The last bastion of rationalism in an insane world ...'

But John's tone seems to be mocking. Ryan can't be sure. His brother was always straightforward. Not like him to take that tone — unless this man is not his brother John.

'We were an élite, remember?' John smiles. 'Sane, scientific approaches to our problems ...'

'All right!'

'What did I say ... ?'

'Nothing.'

'I was only trying to help.'

'I bet you were. You're not my bloody brother. My brother wouldn't — couldn't ...'

'Of course I'm your brother. East Heath Road. Remember East Heath Road where we were born? There was actually a Heath there in those days. Hampstead Heath. There used to be a fair there on Bank Holidays. You must remember that ...'

'But do you?' Ryan looks directly at the man. 'Or are you just very good at learning that sort of information? Eh?'

'Come on, old son ...'

'Leave me alone, you bastard. Leave me alone or I'll ...'

'You'll what?'

'Get out.'

'You'll what?'

'Get out.'

*

117

AFTER THE FAIR WE KIDDED HER . . .
  Q: PLEASE DEFINE SPECIFIC SITUATION
AFTER THE PAIR WE KIDS WERE . . .
  Q: PLEASE DEFINE SPECIFIC SITUATION
AFTER A PEAR WE DID THE . . .
  Q: PLEASE DEFINE SPECIFIC SITUATION
AFTER A LAIR WE RID THE . . .
  Q: PLEASE DEFINE SPECIFIC SITUATION
AFTER THE AFFAIR WE KILLED HER.
*******THANK YOU********************************

*

'NO!'

*

NO	NO	NO	NO		NO
NO	NO	NO	NO		NO
NO O		NO	NO		NO
NONO		NO	NO		NO
NO	NO	NO	NO		NO
NO	NO	NO	NO		NO
NO	NO	NO	NO		NO
NO	N	NO	NONONONO		NONONONO

*

NO!

*

    Ryan rises from his bunk. He is weak, he is trembling. He vomits.
He vomits over the floor of his cabin.
  I need help.
  He staggers from the cabin into the main control room.
  It is empty.
  No one on watch.
  The computer is flashing its signal:
URGENT ATTENTION REQUIRED
URGENT ATTENTION REQUIRED
URGENT ATTENTION REQUIRED.
  He is suspicious of the computer.
  Warily he approaches it.
  The computer says:
*******CONDITION OF OCCUPANTS OF CONTAINERS
NOT******REPORTED"""""""""REPEAT CONDITION OF

OCCUPANTS OF******CONTAINERS NOT REPORTED
""""""""REPORT YOUR OWN******CONDITION******
REPEAT REPORT YOUR OWN CONDITION******LOG
NOT FILED SIXTEEN DAYS""""""""REPEAT LOG NOT
FILED******SIXTEEN DAYS""""""""CONDITION OF
OCCUPANTS OF*********************************

Ryan is astonished.

It is plain to him that whoever else is running the ship, they are not running it as efficiently as he had been doing.

He replies to the computer:

*******OCCUPANTS NO LONGER IN CONTAINERS""""""
MY******OWN CONDITION IS POOR""""""""I HAVE
BEEN OUT OF******OPERATION FOR SIXTEEN DAYS
""""""""WILL FILE REPORTS AS******SOON AS POS-
SIBLE""""""""PLEASE ACKNOWLEDGE***************

He waits for a second. The computer replies.

*******THANK YOU""""""""LOOKING FORWARD TO
HEARING******YOUR LOG ENTRIES""""""""HOWEVER
YOU ARE WRONG ABOUT******OCCUPANTS OF
CONTAINERS""""""""THEY ARE STILL IN******CON-
TAINERS""""""""SORRY TO HEAR YOUR OWN CONDI-
TION******POOR""""""""SUGGEST YOU SWITCH ME TO
FULLY AUTOMATIC******UNTIL YOUR CONDITION
IMPROVES""""""""""DID YOU TAKE********RECOM-
MENDED DOSE PRODITOL""""""""REPEAT DID YOU
TAKE******RECOMMENDED DOSE PRODITOL*******

Ryan is staring incredulously at the second part of the message. Automatically he replies:

******YES I TOOK RECOMMENDED DOSE PRODITOL**
and before the computer replies he leaves the main control room and runs through the dark corridors of the ship until he comes to the hibernation room. He touches the stud and nothing happens. The emergency locks must again be operating. Someone has switched them on.

John?

Or someone pretending to be John?

He runs back to the main control room and switches off the emergency locks, runs back down the corridors to the hibernation room. He opens the door and dashes in.

There they are. As they were when he last saw them. Sleeping in the peace of the hibernation fluid.

Has he imagined . . . ?

No. Someone locked the hibernation room before. Someone

119

locked it again. There is at least one other person aboard. Probably the person posing as John.

He knew there was something odd about him.

An alien aboard.

It is the only explanation.

He realises that he does not remember seeing any of the people together. Doubtless the creature can change shape.

He shudders.

He couldn't have imagined the creature because the Proditol cleared his delusions, at least for a while.

He stares round the hibernation room and he sees the Purdy pistol hanging on the wall. It is odd that it should be here. But providential. He goes to the wall and removes the pistol. It is low on ammunition, but there is some.

He leaves the hibernation room and returns to main control. Hastily he reports on the occupants of the containers.

Then he goes to look for the alien.

Just as he has on his routine inspections, he paces the ship, gun in hand. He checks every cabin, every cabinet, every room.

He finds no one.

He sits down at the desk below the blank TV screen in the main control room and he frowns.

He realises that he has no idea of the characteristics the alien may possess. He could live outside the ship in some ship of his own — attached like a barnacle, perhaps covering the airlock of the *Hope Dempsey*.

The big TV screen above his head is used for scanning the hull. Now he puts it into operation. It scans every inch of the hull. Nothing.

Ryan realises he has eaten virtually nothing for two weeks. That explains his weakness. The creature, he remembers now, never brought him food. He only brought him drugs — and tried, in the shape of his wife Josephine, to administer more. Perhaps it was not Proditol at all . . .

Ryan clutches the back of his neck, massaging it. He holds the gun firmly in his other hand.

There is a polite cough from behind him.

He wheels.

Fred Masterson stands there — or a creature that has assumed the shape of Fred Masterson.

Ryan covers it with his gun, but he does not shoot at once.

'Ryan,' says Fred Masterson. 'You're the only one I can trust. It's Tracy.'

Ryan hears himself saying. 'What about Tracy?'

'I've killed her. I didn't mean to. We were having an argument and — I must have stabbed her. She's dead. She was having an affair with James Henry.'

'What do you intend to do, Fred?'

'I've already done it. But I need your help as commander. I can't hide it from you. I put her in her container. You could say you suggested it. You could tell everybody she needed rest so you suggested she hibernate a little earlier than scheduled.'

Ryan screams at him. 'You're lying! You're lying! What do you know about that?'

'Please help me,' says Masterson. 'Please.'

Ryan fires the pistol, careful not to waste ammunition.

'Masterson' falls.

Ryan smiles. His headache blinds him for a moment. He rubs his eyes.

He goes to see if 'Masterson' is dead.

'Masterson' has vanished. The alien cannot be killed.

Again Ryan feels sick. He feels defeated. He feels impotent.

His headache is worse.

He looks up.

The dancers are there. The group is there. The old woman is there.

Ryan screams and runs out of the control room, down the passage, into his cabin. He seals the cabin door.

He collapses on his bunk.

CHAPTER TWENTY-ONE

Sitting in the sealed cabin, Ryan tries to think things out.

There is no alien aboard. I am merely hallucinating. That is the most obvious explanation.

But it does not explain everything.

It does not explain why the door to the hibernation room was locked.

It does not explain why the Proditol did not work.

He blinks. *Of course. I had no Proditol. I merely deceived myself into believing I had had it. That was why I invented John's sudden awakening.*

And I suppose I could have switched on the emergency locks without realising it.

The strain was too much for me. Some mechanism in my own brain tried to stop me working so hard. It invented the 'help' so that I could relax for a couple of weeks, not worry about running the ship.

Ryan grins with relief. The explanation fits.

And thus I felt guilty about the personnel in the containers. Because I had 'abandoned' them. My talk of their betrayal of me was really my belief that I had betrayed them . . .

Ryan looks down at the gun still clutched in his hand.

He shudders and throws it to the floor.

Uncle Sidney stands near the door.

'You're doing fine, aren't you?' he says.

'Go away, Uncle Sidney. You are an illusion. You are all illusions. Your place is in your container. I'll wake you up when we reach the new planet.' Ryan leans back in his bunk. 'Go on. Off you go.'

'You're a fool,' Uncle Sidney says. 'You've been deceiving yourself all along. Well before you got into this predicament. You were as paranoid as anyone else on Earth. You were just better at rationalising your paranoia, that's all. You don't deserve to have escaped. None of us deserves it. You're clever. But you're all alone now.'

'It's better than having you lot around all the time,' Ryan grins. 'Go on. Get out.'

'It's true,' says Josephine Ryan. 'Uncle Sidney's right. We were humouring you towards the end, you know. It didn't seem to make much difference to me and the boys whether we went up in an H-bomb attack or up in a spaceship. In a way I think I'd have preferred the H-bomb. I wouldn't have had to listen to your self-righteous pronouncements day in and day out until you . . .'

'Until I what?'

'Until . . .'

'Go on. Say it!' Ryan laughs in her face. 'Go on, Jo — say it!'

'Until I went into hibernation.'

'Bloody shrinking violet!' Ryan sneers at her. 'If I'd have had a stronger woman . . .'

'You needed one,' she says. 'I'll admit that.'

'Shut up.'

'You got rid of the strong one, didn't you?' says Fred Masterson. 'Did her in, eh?'

'Shut up!'

'Just like you did James Henry in,' says Janet Ryan, 'after you helped Fred cover up Tracy's death. Shot him in the control room with that gun, didn't you?'

'Shut up!'

'You got worse and worse,' says John Ryan. 'We tried to help you. We put you under sedation. We humoured you. But you had to do it, didn't you?'

'Do what? Tell me?'

'Put me in hibernation,' says John Ryan.

Ryan laughs. 'You, too?'

Ida and Felicity Henry laugh harshly. Ida's hands are folded over her swollen abdomen. 'You lost all your friends, didn't you, Ryan?' says Felicity. 'You sold yourself the alien story, didn't you, in the end? After being so scornful about it, you swallowed it when you could least afford to.'

'Shut up. You'll go, too.'

'You've got us all in hibernation,' says James Henry. 'But we can still talk to you. We'll be able to talk to you again, when we wake up.'

Ryan laughs.

'What are you laughing about, dad?' says Alexander Ryan.

'Let us in on it, dad. Go on!' says Rupert Ryan.

Ryan stops laughing. He clears his throat.

'Out you go, boys,' he says. 'You don't want to be involved in this.'

'But we are involved,' says Alex. 'It's not our fault our dad's a silly old fart.'

'She turned you against me,' says Ryan.

'Anyone can see you're a silly old fart, dad,' Rupert says reasonably.

'I did my best for you,' Ryan says. 'I gave you everything.'

'Everything?' says Josephine. She sniffs.

'Things will be different on the new planet. I'll have time for you and the boys.' He tone is placatory. 'I had so much work to do. So many plans to make. I had to be so careful.'

'And you were.' Isabel Ryan winks at him. 'Weren't you?'

'You'd better shut up, Isobel. I warned you before to keep your mouth shut about that . . .'

He glances at Janet. Janet bursts out laughing. 'I slept with you because I was shit scared of you,' she says.

'Shut up!'

'I was afraid you'd do it to me, too.'

'Do what?' He dares her. 'What?'

She looks at the floor. 'Put me in hibernation,' she murmurs.

123

Ryan sneers at them all. 'Not one with guts, is there? You all wanted to get rid of me. You all thought you could plan behind my back. But you forgot' — he taps his head — 'I've got brains — I'm rational — I worked it out scientifically — pragmatically ... I used a system, didn't I? And I beat you *all*!'

'You didn't get me,' says Tracy Masterson.

Ryan screams.

CHAPTER TWENTY-TWO

Ryan is better now.

The hallucinations have passed. Some dreams still disturb him, but not seriously.

He paces the spaceship. He paces down the central passageway to the main control cabin and there he checks the coordinates, the consumption indicators, the regeneration indicators and he checks all his figures, at length, with those of the ship's computer.

Everything is perfectly in order; exactly as it should be.

Near the ship's big central screen is a desk. Although activated the screen shows no picture, but it casts a greenish light on to the desk. Ryan sits down and depresses a stud on the small console on his desk. In a clear, level voice he makes his standard log entry.

'Day number one thousand, four hundred and ninety. Spaceship *Hope Dempsey* en route for Munich 15040. Speed holds steady at point nine of c. All systems functioning according to original expectations. No other variations. We are all comfortable.

'Signing off.

'Ryan, Commander.'

Ryan now slides open a drawer and takes from it a large red book. It is a new book, with only one page filled in. He enters the date and underlines it in red.

He writes:

Another day without much to report. I am a little depressed, but I felt worse yesterday and I think my spirits are improving. I am rather lonely and sometimes wish I could wake someone else up so that we could talk a little together. But that would be unwise. I persevere. I keep myself mentally active and physically fit. It's my duty.

All the horror and humiliation and wretchedness of Earth is far behind us. We shall be starting a new race, soon. And the world we'll build will be a cleaner world. A sane world. A world built according to knowledge and sanity — not fear and guilt.

Ryan finished his entry and neatly puts his book away.

The computer is flashing at him.

He goes over to it and reads.

REPORT ON PERSONNEL IN CONTAINERS NOT SUPPLIED.

A stupid oversight. Ryan punches in the reports:

JOSEPHINE RYAN.	CONDITION STEADY
RUPERT RYAN.	CONDITION STEADY
ALEXANDER RYAN.	CONDITION STEADY
SIDNEY RYAN.	CONDITION STEADY
JOHN RYAN.	CONDITION STEADY
ISABEL RYAN.	CONDITION STEADY
JANET RYAN.	CONDITION STEADY
FRED MASTERSON.	CONDITION STEADY

He hesitates for a moment, then he continues:

TRACY MASTERSON.	CONDITION STEADY
JAMES HENRY.	CONDITION STEADY
IDA HENRY.	CONDITION STEADY
FELICITY HENRY.	CONDITION STEADY*******

****
*******YOUR OWN CONDITION

suggests the computer.

Ryan shrugs.

CONDITION STEADY

he reports.

*

Ryan sleeps.

He is in the ballroom. It is dusk and long windows look out on to a darkening lawn.

Formally dressed couples slowly rotate in perfect time to the music, which is low and sombre. All the couples have round, very black glasses hiding their eyes. Their pale faces are almost invisible in the dim light . . .

Ryan awakes. He smiles, wondering what the dream can mean.

He gets up and stretches. For some reason he remembers old Owen Powell, the man he had to dismiss, the man who killed himself. That gave him a bad turn at the time. Still . . .

He dismisses the thought. No point in dwelling on the past when the future's so much more important.

He switches on the agriculture programme. Might just as well do a bit of homework until he can get back to sleep.

He falls asleep in front of the screen.

*

The spacecraft moves through the silence of the cosmos. It moves so slowly as to seem not to move at all.

It is a lonely little object.

*

Space is infinite.
It is dark.
Space is neutral.
It is cold.

THE END

MICHAEL MOORCOCK—MAYFLOWER SCIENCE FANTASY

The Cornelius Chronicles

The Adventures of Una Persson and Catherine Cornelius in the Twentieth Century	£1.25	☐

The Dancers at the End of Time

An Alien Heat	95p	☐
The Hollow Lands	£1.25	☐
The End of All Songs	£1.25	☐

Hawkmoon: The History of the Runestaff

The Jewel in the Skull	£1.25	☐
The Mad God's Amulet	95p	☐
The Sword of the Dawn	£1.25	☐
The Runestaff	95p	☐

Hawkmoon: The Chronicles of Castle Brass

Count Brass	£1.25	☐
The Champion of Garathorm	95p	☐
The Quest for Tanelorn	£1.25	☐

Erekosë

The Eternal Champion	95p	☐
Phoenix in Obsidian	£1.25	☐

Elric

The Sailor on the Seas of Fate	95p	☐

All these books are available at your local bookshop or newsagent, or can be ordered direct from the publisher. Just tick the titles you want and fill in the form below.

Name _____

Address _____

_____

Write to Granada Cash Sales
PO Box 11, Falmouth, Cornwall TR10 9EN.

Please enclose remittance to the value of the cover price plus:

UK 45p for the first book, 20p for the second book plus 14p per copy for each additional book ordered to a maximum charge of £1.63.

BFPO and Eire 45p for the first book, 20p for the second book plus 14p per copy for the next 7 books, thereafter 8p per book.

Overseas 75p for the first book and 21p for each additional book.

Granada Publishing reserve the right to show new retail prices on covers, which may differ from those previously advertised in the text or elsewhere.

SF1181